Amy Cross is the author of more than 250 horror, paranormal, fantasy and thriller novels.

THE HAUNTING OF MARLSTONE HALL

THE GHOSTS OF ROSE RADCLIFFE BOOK 2

AMY CROSS

CONTENTS

THE HAUNTING OF MARLSTONE HALL

CHAPTER ONE

"PEOPLE WHO BELIEVE IN ghosts are pathetic," Daniel said once the desserts had been set down on the dining table. "Let's be honest and call a spade a spade here. Anyone who believes in ghosts is... intellectually challenged, to say the least. They're complete morons. Imbeciles."

"That's a little harsh," Rebecca Pearson suggested as she sat back down.

"Is it?" Daniel replied, turning to her with his glass of wine still in his hand. He'd already spilled several drops on the white tablecloth. "Really? Why do we coddle these people? Why do we even give them the time of day? I'd have thought that you of all people would recognize that I'm telling the truth. Given that little hobby you and

Jonathan took up a while ago, that is."

"I agree that the idea of ghosts is... ludicrous," she told him, choosing her words with care since she knew that Daniel tended to latch onto even the tiniest of mistakes like a deranged terrier, "but that doesn't mean that the belief in them is inherently -"

"*Mistaken* belief," Daniel added abruptly, clearly feeling a very urgent need to correct her.

"A mistaken belief is still of interest from an academic standpoint," she continued. "Why do people believe in ghosts when they're clearly not real? Who do they ignore evidence and concoct wild stories? Why do they sometimes even try to falsify evidence of the paranormal? What social issues are driving such people to such extreme efforts?"

"They're idiots," Daniel said firmly, before turning to look at the other end of the table. "No more, no less. And these days, you've got the added lure of social media. Every halfwit's desperate for a video that'll go viral, and what's better than some nonsense about the undead? You agree with me, Jonathan, don't you?"

"Rebecca and I have conducted almost a dozen investigations into supposed hauntings recently," Jonathan said cautiously, watching his wife carefully for a moment. "Every single time, we've been able to explain what's really going on. Sometimes the people involved genuinely believe that they're experiencing paranormal events and sometimes they're motivated by baser instincts. Money's one factor, plus – as you said – social media and online fame can be powerful drugs. But Rebecca is right when she suggests that there are often complex psychological issues at play here."

He turned to Roger Packham, who was sitting on the other side of the table.

"Roger?"

"Hmm?" Roger replied, having been daydreaming a little.

"You agree, don't you?" Jonathan continued, briefly removing his glasses and cleaning them using the bottom of his shirt. "That claims of hauntings are worth studying, albeit purely through the lens of social studies and so on?"

"That sounds about right," Roger told him. "Sorry, I must confess that my mind wandered a little there. I was thinking about something else entirely. How very rude of me."

"Poor Roger can't even be bothered to listen to us prattling on about this nonsense," Daniel suggested, before taking another sip of wine.

Already, his lips were stained slightly red.

"I don't blame him, either. To be honest, Jonathan, I'm surprised that you even deign to look into these claims." He paused for a moment with a slightly mischievous smile on his lips. "Then again, women tend to be more gullible when it comes to such matters. Are you sure you're not just indulging your wife with these extracurricular investigations?"

"Don't be ridiculous," Rebecca sighed, rolling her eyes.

"Let's all calm down a little," Jonathan said, putting his glasses back on before looking at each of his guests in turn. He knew how easily Daniel could cause a good mood to turn sour. "We don't hold these dinner parties so that we can argue. We hold them so that we can discuss important matters relating to our overlapping fields of study at the university. Rigorous debate is one thing, but I don't want things getting too heated. Don't forget that fundamentally we're all on the same side, and that side stands for truth in all aspects of our work."

"Mummy?"

Startled, Rebecca turned to see her daughter standing in the doorway, holding her favorite teddy bear.

"I can't sleep," Alicia said, although she certainly looked and sounded tired. "I've tried and

I've tried but... I just can't. And Mr. Anderson's the same."

She held her bear up.

"He thought we should come down and ask if you can settle us in again. I told him we probably shouldn't disturb you but... well, kept insisting."

"I think perhaps we've been too loud," Rebecca said, setting her napkin down before getting to her feet and heading over to the girl. "I was worried about that. Sweetheart, I'll take you back up, and then we'll be much quieter for the rest of the evening." She turned and glared at her husband. "Isn't that right, Jonathan?"

"That's right," he replied, briefly raising his glass to her as she left the room, then taking another sip.

"I really don't know why you humor her silly ideas," Daniel said once he was sure that Rebecca was out of earshot. "Didn't you find your little trips to be a complete waste of time?"

"Actually I found them interesting," Jonathan replied, "and Rebecca and I are really on the same page when it comes to such things. We both know that ghosts and the supernatural aren't real. And we hoped that by debunking such claims we could help people to look past those fantasies and accept whatever's really going on in their lives.

Anyway, it's all in the past now. We decided to stop doing that sort of work. We're both far too busy."

***

"Daniel's not staying too much longer, is he?"

"Probably not," Jonathan muttered half an hour later, standing in the kitchen and watching as his wife refreshed the cheeseboard. "I'm sorry, I know he can be acerbic sometimes, but he means well."

"Does he?"

"I swear. You just don't know him as well as I do, that's all."

"I'm probably just overreacting," she replied. "After all, I'm a mere woman. We tend to get overly emotional about things."

At this, Jonathan sighed.

"It's not supposed to be my time of the month quite yet," she added, "but I suppose it might be coming a little early and -"

"Alright, I get it," he sighed. "I completely get it."

"I just can't believe that a-hole," she continued, cutting some brie into slices with a little more determination than before. "Does he really not see any value in the work we do? Does he really think that we just go running around to various old houses for a laugh?"

"Daniel says things to get a reaction," Jonathan told her. "You know that."

"He's liable to get a reaction, alright," she muttered. "And that reaction will be the rolling pin getting shoved up his -"

"Let's just keep things civil," Jonathan replied, heading over and stopping next to her, then putting a hand on the side of her arm. "We're both going to be very busy with our new projects for a while, so it's not even as if we'll have time to debunk more ghost stories. Certainly not in the near future. We agreed to put the kibosh on it all for now, remember? That's probably a good thing."

"Maybe."

"Did Alicia settle?"

"She did, but I told you it wasn't a good idea to host the latest dinner party here. Daniel's voice is so loud, they can probably hear him on the other side of the town."

"Do you want me to talk to him? I can try to make him go easy on you."

"No, don't do that. He'll just make more of his stupid jokes."

"Is something else bothering you?" he asked. "You've seemed a little off all day and I can't help worrying that something's on your mind."

"It's nothing," she told him, before hesitating as she realized that she could never hide anything from her husband. Not for long, anyway. "I worry about Alicia sometimes. She doesn't have many friends."

"She's fine," he countered. "The teachers say she's doing brilliantly in school."

"At her academic subjects, sure," she replied, "but what about other things? What about... life?"

"I didn't have any friends when I was her age, and I turned out fine."

She raised a skeptical eyebrow.

"Personally I'd be worried if she was making a load of fake friends," he muttered. "She's still in primary school, and statistically speaking most people lose touch with primary school friends anyway. In a few years from now she'll hopefully be at St. Edmund's and then I'm sure she'll make more than enough friends. And of course she'll have to focus on her studies if she wants to become a doctor."

"*Does* she want to become a doctor?"

"Or whatever she decides to do with her life," he suggested, before squeezing her arm. "You're her mother, so it's natural that you're worried, but just let her grow up the way she wants to, okay?"

"You don't think she's lonely, do you?"

He opened his mouth to reply, but in that moment he heard a set of footsteps hurrying through. From the pace and clumsiness of those footsteps, he immediately knew that Daniel was on the hunt – no doubt for more wine, or more cheese, or most likely both.

"There you are!" Daniel said as he made his way into the room and set his empty wine glass down. "I've just been explaining to old Roger why he's go utterly wrong about Antrobe's new theory. The guy's really set in his ways, though, and he keeps wittering on about margins of error and all that stuff. Jonathan, do you think you can try to drum it into his stupid old head that there might be some newer methodologies that apply here?"

"Actually, Rebecca's more of an expert on that stuff than I am," Jonathan replied.

"Sure," Daniel said, "but... I don't know, I just think you have a way of... sounding more convincing when you're explaining things. No offense, Rebecca."

After glaring at him for a moment, Rebecca slowly reached for the rolling pin. At the last second, however, Jonathan gently put a hand on her wrist in order to hold her back.

"Rebecca's definitely the person for the job," he said firmly, before turning to her. "Darling, why don't you go and let poor Roger down gently? Meanwhile Daniel and I will finish up the cheeseboard and bring it through shortly."

CHAPTER TWO

"SMUG, ARROGANT -"

Stopping as soon as she entered the study, Rebecca sighed.

"Sorry," she added, forcing a smile as she saw Roger leafing though one of the journals on the desk. "Ignore me. I'm just tired."

"Finding Daniel to be a tad grating, are you?" he asked. "Join the club. To be honest, I don't even know why Jonathan insists on inviting him to these get-togethers every month. The man's a complete ass. I know of half a dozen very learned colleagues who'd be only to happy to come to our soirees if only they could be assured that a certain Mr. Brown wasn't going to show up. The man is a room-clearer. A pub-clearer. Hell, there aren't many places he *can't* clear with that motormouth of his."

"He's giving me a headache," she admitted.

"Again, join the club," he admitted. "I find that whenever I'm in danger of sharing a room with Daniel Brown for more than a few minutes, a couple of paracetamol help to take the edge off and make him at least slightly bearable."

"Lesson learned," she told him, feeling slightly relieved that he at least seemed to understand her predicament. That was more than her husband had managed, at least. "I'm sorry, I haven't had much of a chance to ask you this evening. How's your work going?"

"Oh, it's rumbling along," he replied. "Funding's a bitch and I can't find a decent assistant. The usual complaints. How about yours?"

"I'm making some progress."

"And what about the side project?" he added, turning to her with a knowing stare. "What about the ghost investigations and the debunkings and all that?"

"It's been months since we did one," she told him. "To be honest, I think after twelve we might be done. It was a fun side project but... nothing more than that."

"Twelve, eh?" he muttered. "So if you did another one, that'd be thirteen, would it?"

"I suppose so."

"Interesting." He continued to flick through the journal for a few more seconds, before setting it down and turning to her. "I must admit, when Jonathan first told me that the pair of you were going to turn into part-time ghost-hunters -"

"Paranormal investigators," she said quickly, correcting him.

"I'm sorry, paranormal investigators... Well, I was surprised. I know your plan was always to investigate the reasons why people make such claims, but did you never even once stop to consider the possibility that you might encounter something you wouldn't be able to explain?"

"No," she said confidently. "Never."

"And during the course of your investigations, were there ever times – even very briefly – in which you questioned whether you might be wrong?"

"No," she said again.

"Because..."

"Because Jonathan and I both know that ghosts and the paranormal don't exist. That was our starting point and we've had no trouble sticking to it. We've been to twelve houses and investigated twelve so-called hauntings, and we've shown them all to be nothing of the sort."

"Yes, and that's not a bad sample size," he admitted, "but..."

She waited for him to continue, but she could tell now that something was troubling him. Roger Packham was one of the most brilliant men she'd ever met, and she knew he certainly wasn't given to mindless idle speculation. Everyone at the university was fully aware that when Roger talked, it was wise to pay attention.

"Have you ever heart of Martin Delaney?" he asked finally.

"Of course. He used to work in your department, didn't he?"

"That's the fellow," he said with a faint, sad smile. "Always wore a bow-tie. Fond of striped trousers. Confirmed bachelor, loved cricket. That sort of thing. He died not too long ago, actually, at the terribly young age of just fifty-five. That's not old these days, is it? Then again, cancer isn't a great respecter of decency. Poor bastard."

"I was sorry to hear about that."

"Martin used to dabble in what you're dabbling in," he continued. "Did you know that?"

"Of course. Everyone knew that he was the king of paranormal investigations. He couldn't be tricked or fooled, not by anyone or anything. Even master magicians found they couldn't get anything past him. He was one of the inspirations for our own work, actually."

She waited for a reply, but now he was simply watching her.

"He had a one hundred per cent success record," she added. "Like Jonathan and me, actually."

"He went off on a few ghost-hunts of his own," he explained, "and he always managed to figure out what was going on. *Always*. At least, that's what he used to tell everyone. But in his quieter moments, when he'd had a drink or two and he knew he was with good friends, he'd sometimes admit – toward the end – that there was one case that had... eluded him. One that he'd never quite managed to solve."

"I find that hard to believe," she told him with a nervous smile. "Martin Delaney was one of the most brilliant minds of his generation. There's no way he wouldn't be able to figure out something as simple as a supposed haunting."

"Yet that's exactly what happened," Roger said, and now he had a slight twinkle in his eye. "Tell me, have you ever heard of Marlstone Hall?"

***

"She's sleeping," Jonathan said, keeping his voice low as he pulled the bedroom door shut a few hours later. "Damn it, I can't believe we finally managed to get rid of Daniel. I swear the guy could talk for England. That poor bloody taxi driver's ears'll be bleeding by the time he gets back to Oxford."

He checked his watch.

"Two in the morning," he continued. "That's a record, even for him. I don't think I've been up drinking until two in the morning since my student days. I'm going to feel it in the morning, that's for sure."

"Have you ever heard of Marlstone Hall?"

Furrowing his brow, he turned to see that Rebecca was still taking off her make-up as she continued to get ready for bed.

"Where?" he asked.

"It's in West Yorkshire," she explained, keeping an eye on his reflection in the mirror. "Near Dewsbury, as it happens. Not that I've ever been to Dewsbury, but there you go. Marlstone Hall is one of those big old English houses that are left over from the days when men vied to build country piles that might impress the royals. They tied to outdo each other in terms of size, girth, that sort of thing. It's basically out in the middle of nowhere and apparently now it's used primarily as a tourist attraction. Or at least, that's the theory. I checked out the website just now, but to be honest it doesn't seem to have much to offer."

"Sounds fascinating," he replied as he pulled his tie off and began to unbutton his shirt. "Sounds like any one of hundreds, maybe thousands, of useless old country houses that are dotted all over the English countryside."

"One of the supposed selling points of the place is that it's said to be haunted."

"I bet they love telling that story on the guided tours."

"I'm sure they do," she said, still watching him in the mirror as she tried to work out whether she might be making a terrible mistake. "Do you remember how Martin Delaney used to go around investigating haunted houses, pretty much the same way that we've been doing?"

"Of course. He was always one step ahead of us."

"According to Roger, he debunked Highbridge Priory in three days. That one took us almost a week."

"Okay, but -"

"And he debunked Cretchingham Windmill in two days. We spent a long weekend there."

"Sure, and -"

"And do you remember the four days it took us to prove that Witchimore Castle isn't haunted?"

"Yes, but -"

"That one took him an afternoon," she added pointedly. "The guy was clearly a genius. By all accounts there wasn't a haunted house, hall, windmill, castle or any other structure that he couldn't walk into and resolve. And I don't mean to puncture your ego here, but he seems to have been... better at it than we are."

"Ouch," he said with deadpan humor. "Shoot me again, why don't you?"

"But Marlstone Hall outfoxed him," she continued, finally turning to face him directly as he sat on the edge of the bed and began to pull off his socks. "Apparently even on his deathbed he was talking about it. He spent two weeks there trying to prove that the place isn't haunted, but instead... he gathered evidence to the contrary."

"He proved that it *is* haunted?"

"Hard to say exactly," she replied, "because apparently one of his last acts was to burn every document and photograph from his investigation into the place. Even his diaries. And he didn't talk about it much, but when he was alone with people he trusted... he was willing to admit that Marlstone Hall was stuck in his mind. Whatever he saw or encountered there, he was never able to explain it. At least, that's what Roger claims."

"And you're bringing this up now because... what, exactly?"

"You and I have investigated twelve haunted houses and solved them all," she pointed out. "Don't you think that the ideal way to round off our little side career as ghost-hunters would be to solve the one case that Martin Delaney never could? Or try to, at least. Wouldn't that be the perfect way to shut someone like Daniel Brown up forever?"

"I thought we agreed -"

"One more case, Jonathan," she continued, getting to her feet. "That's all I'm asking. Let's do one big, final case just to really prove to ourselves that we've got what it takes. And if we can do something that Martin Delaney couldn't, then we'll be able to hold our heads high. We've never backed down from a challenge, not once. Let's not do it now."

"You're really serious, aren't you?" he replied.

"I want to show losers like Daniel Brown that we mean business," she said firmly. "Besides, thirteen cases sounds like a way more fitting number than twelve. What do you say? Are you up for one last job?"

CHAPTER THREE

"MUMMY AND DADDY WILL be home really soon," Rebecca said over the phone a few weeks later, as she sat in the car's passenger seat and watched the West Yorkshire countryside flashing past. "Just be good for Nana Evelyn, okay? I don't want to get home and find out that you've been causing trouble."

"I won't cause trouble," Alicia replied over the phone, "but I don't get why I couldn't come with you."

"You know Daddy and I sometimes have to go away for work," she pointed out. "But if it makes you feel any better, this really *will* be the last time. I promise."

"Do you really?"

"Of course," she said, before briefly spotting a large gray building in the distance.

The place was quickly lost again behind a wall of trees.

"But we're about to arrive, so I'm going to have to get off the phone. Tell Nana Evelyn that I love her, and that you're going to be really well behaved for her all weekend. Do we have a deal?"

"Okay," Alicia said cautiously, although she sounded far from convinced. "I wish you'd let me go with you sometimes, though. I'd like to have adventures too. I'm ten years old! It's not fair that I always have to stay at home!"

"She's missing us," Rebecca said once she'd cut the call and had slipped her phone into her bag. "I suppose that's better than the alternative."

"We're nearly there," Jonathan replied, slowing the car and turning onto a bumpy private road that led into the forest.

"I think I saw the place briefly."

"You did," he continued. "You know, I still can't quite believe that we're all the way out here in West Yorkshire. This is a long way to come just to prove a point."

"It's a point work proving again and again," she replied, "until certain people get it into their thick skulls. I know we initially conducted these little ghost-hunts more for our own amusement, Jonathan, but now I really think we should think about writing them all up into some kind of study. We've learned so much about the reasons people falsely claim to have experienced these things. We've taken an unserious subject and turned it into a teachable moment."

"If you want to take the lead on that, then be my guest," he muttered as he steered the car around a tight bend. "As for me, I meant what I said when you first proposed this trip. I'm doing it mainly so that you can feel some kind of finality about the whole project. I'm completely serious, Rebecca. This is our last ever haunted house investigation."

***

"It's certainly stately," Rebecca said a few minutes later, climbing out of the car and swinging the door shut, before taking a few steps forward across the gravel driveway. "I'm not sure how homely it is, though. How old is it, again?"

"Marlstone Hall was built in 1769 for Sir Gillies Marlstone," Jonathan replied, reading from the tourist leaflet as he made his way round to join her. "It was sold to the Wingham family in 1827, then to the Wilkinsons in 1911 – and they ran it as an orphanage. After that it was briefly put into service as a home for evacuated children during the Second World War, and then it was purchased by a construction company that used it as their headquarters until it was sold again in 1985, this time to the Sinclair family. When they fell on hard times a few years ago, they decided to try to turn the place into a tourist attraction with a sideline in boutique weekend stays and big fancy weddings."

He turned the leaflet over.

"Entry is fifteen pounds per adult," he added, "or nine pounds for children. Anyone under seven years of age can go in for free. No dogs except guide dogs. There's a -"

"Okay, that's enough background for now," she said, interrupting him. "This place seems to have a real patchwork quilt of a history. I doubt I'll remember half of what you just told me. But you let them know that we were coming, right?"

"The woman I spoke to was only too keen," he replied with a faint smile, holding up the leaflet to reveal a photo of a corridor complete with an obviously fake ghostly figure. "Apparently they even do entire ghost weekends. When they don't end up having to cancel them due to lack of interest, that is. I'd have thought that would be a more lucrative market."

"Aren't they worried that we could ruin that side of it all for them?" she asked as they made their way toward the steps at the front of the building.

"I think Martin Delaney's failure emboldened them," he suggested. "They've plastered his name all over their website, claiming that England's foremost paranormal investigator was unable to disprove their claims. To be honest, I get it. If they can charge unsuspecting fools several hundred pounds for a supposedly ghostly weekend, why shouldn't they give it a try?"

"Because it's a complete lie," she pointed out.

"That wouldn't make it the first profitable enterprise built on untruths and falsehoods," he suggested, stopping at the top of the steps to look around at the large gardens surrounding the house. "It must cost an absolute fortune to keep a place like this running. Think of the electricity bill alone, and that's before you even think about trying to do it up or maintain the lawns. I bet they need every penny they can get their hands on."

"We certainly do."

Turning, Rebecca and Jonathan saw a tall, dark-haired woman emerging from the front door with her hand already outstretched and a red-lipped smile on her face.

"You must be the Pearsons," she said, shaking Jonathan's hand first and then Rebecca's a moment later. "I'm Ida Sinclair. Don't worry, I'm not going to pretend to be psychic. It's just that you're the only guests we've got booked in for this weekend, so I hazarded an educated guess. Do you not have any luggage with you?"

"We've got a suitcase in the car," he told her.

"Then why don't you bring it inside while I give your wife a little guided tour?" she replied, before taking Rebecca by the arm and leading her over to the door. "What's the use in having a husband if they're not going to do the heavy lifting?" she added with a smile. "After my dear Henry died a few years ago, I was shocked to realize just how hard it is to get things done without a man at your side. I know that's not terribly politically correct in 2011, but one has to speak the truth, doesn't one?"

"I -"

"But I learned," Ida continued, evidently in no mood to let her speech become a full-blown back-and-forth conversation just yet. "I rolled my sleeves up and I assembled a small team to keep us going through the high season. Of course, at this time of year they're all surplus to requirements so I release them to pursue alternative employment in the area. They almost always come back the following spring, though. Their loyalty to me is quite remarkable."

"So how many people do you have working here right now?" Rebecca asked, before glancing over her shoulder and seeing Jonathan struggling to pull the suitcase out of the car.

"None whatsoever," Ida said, leading her into the grand entrance hallway and stopping beneath the chandelier. "It's simple enough," she added, turning to her guest. "We seal up the vast majority of the place every October or November, and we keep it that way until March or April. That leaves us with a rather cozy little house-within-a-house, so to speak, and we're delightfully happy."

"We?"

"My daughter and I," Ida explained. "She's only eight years old, but she has a good head on her shoulders. I've taken to home-schooling her because, well, frantically it's far more convenient. The two of us potter about and keep things going, and I plan for the next season. Marlstone Hall has something of a life of its own, you see. I swear the place spies on me and tries to work out the worst moment to burst a pipe or develop a hole in its roof. I can't even begin to tell you how much it costs to keep the building rattling along for even a single day. The whole process has certainly been an eyeopener."

Glancing past her host, Rebecca saw Jonathan struggling inside with the suitcase.

"There you go," Ida called out to him with a smile. "I knew you could do it eventually. Make sure not to scuff the skirting boards, though. I only had them touched up last year."

"Do you by any chance have a lift?" he asked slightly breathlessly.

"I'm afraid not," she replied, clearly enjoying his struggles, "so you'll just have to put your back into it. You seem like a stocky fellow, I'm sure you'll manage. I've put you in the Argylle Suite, it's at the top of the stairs and just to the left. Meanwhile your wife and I shall go through to the dining room and establish the terms of your little weekend engagement here at the house."

Taking hold of Rebecca's arm, she began to lead her along a nearby corridor.

"I'm terribly excited to have you here," she explained as their voices drifted away from the entrance hall. "You know what they say, any publicity is good publicity. And the last fellow who came here and tried to poo-poo the whole thing ended up running away with his tail between his legs, if you know what I mean."

"Right," Jonathan said, still standing next to the suitcase as he looked at the ominous staircase ahead. "Let's see about finding this Argylle Suite, shall we? Can't be too hard."

He began to pull the suitcase across the hallway, only to wince and stop as he felt a sharp pain in the small of his back. He waited a few more seconds, and then – fairly confident now that the pain was gone – he set off again.

CHAPTER FOUR

"IT'S REALLY BEAUTIFUL," REBECCA said as she stepped into the study and looked around at the vast number of bookshelves, all of which were heaving under the weight of so many dusty old volumes. "You've got your own little library here."

"We do indeed," Ida replied, wandering to one of the shelves and pulling out a book, taking a moment to wipe dust from the top. "Pick your subject and I'm sure we have some of the finest reference works, not to mention the most revered works of western literature. And a smattering of classics from further afield, of course. Most of them haven't been touched since they were delivered."

She opened the book, causing the spine to creak loudly.

"I found a wonderful little website that sells

them en masse," she added with a faint smile, as if she was proud of her little scheme. "Five thousand books arrived all in one go. They're on a wide variety of topics and, frankly, I'm not much of a reader. But the room looked so bare without them. Fortunately they have different tiers, so you can make sure that you're not taking delivery of pure dross. You pay by weight, essentially."

"Book by the kilo, huh?" Rebecca replied, quickly realizing that she probably shouldn't be surprised – or judgmental. "You've certainly put a lot of work in."

"People come to an old English country hall and they expect certain... props," Ida told her. "Most of the time they've never been to a place like Marlstone Hall before but they've watched the usual television shows so they think they know what to expect. It's all rather theatrical and -"

Before she could finish, they both heard a loud bump coming from somewhere above.

Looking up, Rebecca saw a small chandelier hanging from the ceiling.

"I'm not going to try to pretend that was a ghost," Ida said after a moment, with a trace of weary resignation in her voice. "My daughter is... somewhere in the place. She's young and somewhat difficult to control at times, although I suppose no more so than the average child. Do you have any offspring of your own?"

"One," Rebecca replied, turning to her again. "A girl. She's ten."

"My Rose is eight," Ida continued. "People keep saying that it's such a lovely age, but to be honest I'm looking forward to her growing up just a little. She'll be more useful around the place."

"Your website mentions a ghost," Rebecca said, keen to get to the subject at hand. "It's not hugely clear what kind of ghost you believe you have here."

"Well, I thought that was *your* job to determine," Ida replied, once again smiling slightly. "I wouldn't want to try to influence you in any way, so I think it's best if you go about your investigation without any preconceptions."

"But you believe..."

Rebecca hesitated, wondering exactly how to phrase her next question.

"Do you actually believe that Marlstone Hall is haunted," she continued finally, "or is it all just a bit of a... story... to try to drum up business?"

"You're asking me if I'm a liar?"

"That's not exactly what I meant."

Now it was Ida's turn to hesitate, before slowly reaching over and sliding the book back into the shelf and then taking a moment to wipe away some more dust from the adjacent volumes.

"There *is* a ghost here, Mrs. Pearson," she said after a few more seconds had passed. "Perhaps more than one, I wouldn't like to be too specific. But there is most certainly a presence, of that I have no doubt. Martin... I mean, Mr. Delaney was here not that long ago and he was quite unable to disprove that claim. I am quite sure that you will come to the same conclusion."

"My husband and I tend to work from a skeptical starting point."

"So did Mr. Delaney," Ida continued with a smile. "By the time he left, however, the poor man was rather shaken. I imagine he saw the same ghostly apparition that several people have reported over the years, and it shook him to his core. If you don't believe in such things, Mrs. Pearson, then I might caution you to prepare yourself. Marlstone Hall *is* haunted, and you'll find that our for yourself soon enough. And when you do, I look forward to adding some quotes from you and your husband to our promotional literature. I've already had several potential mock-ups prepared."

***

"What do you think?"

Having found her husband in the dining room, Rebecca saw that he was looking at various old plates that had been put on display in a case at the far end. She could only assume that – like her – he was somewhat bemused by the fact that

Marlstone Hall was simultaneously so frightfully grand and so desperately rundown. For every chandelier or grand dining table, there were countless cracks in the walls and spots of chipped plaster.

"Found anything?" she continued, stepping into the room.

"Dust," he replied, wiping a fingertip across the top of a shelf and then examining the conglomeration of matter he'd collected on a fingertip. "Lots and lots of dust."

"Mrs. Sinclair thought it best if we take a look around for ourselves," she said as she headed over to join him. "She certainly seems very confident that we're going to come around to her way of thinking. My first impression of her is that she's very subtle with her performance."

"Performance?"

"She knows what people want in a place like this and she gives it to them," she continued, looking up at the high ceiling. "Or she tries to, to the best of her ability and within her budget. She dropped a few hints about nightfall and strange noises, and I could tell that she was studying my every reaction. My first thought is that she might be quite manipulative."

"Have you met the daughter yet?"

"Not yet, but I've heard her," Rebecca admitted, stopping behind one of the chairs and giving it a gentle push, feeling its solid frame. "You don't think *she's* the ghost, do you?"

"Hardly," Jonathan replied. "I've got to be honest, so far the place doesn't exactly have a very foreboding atmosphere. It's quite light, really." He turned and looked over toward some paintings on the far side of the room. "It's not much of a tourist attraction, either. If I'd shown up and paid money to have a look around, I'd be feeling rather short-changed by now. Is there even a tearoom?"

"I'm sure it's more impressive when the whole house is open," she suggested. "The part we're in now is barely a quarter of it."

"I'm still underwhelmed," he replied. "I can't help thinking that we'll be done here inside of a day."

"Just like Martin Delaney wasn't?" she pointed out.

"Martin was a genius, but even geniuses have bad days in the office," he countered. "And don't forget that the man was ill by that point. His judgment might have been clouded, so never take anything for granted. Just because he got a lot of things right, you can't assume that he didn't... fall apart once he got to this particular house. If he knew he was dying by the time he rocked up at Marlstone Hall... his mind might not have been quite so sharp."

"Yes, well I suppose that's a good -"

Before she could finish, she heard a scraping sound coming from the other end of the room. She turned and looked over at the open doorway, and a moment later a young girl stepped into view, partially hiding behind the jamb.

"Hello, there, " Rebecca said with a smile, taking a few steps around the table so that she could see the girl a little better, "and what's your name? Hang on a minute, you must be Mrs. Sinclair's daughter. Your name's Rose, isn't it?"

The girl hesitated, before slowly and very cautiously entering the room.

"You live in a nice big house, Rose," Rebecca continued, heading over to her and holding out a hand. "I don't know how much your mother has told you, but I'm Rebecca Pearson and this is my husband Jonathan. We're here to... look around your house for the weekend."

With her hand still outstretched, she waited for Rose to respond.

"How do you do?" the girl replied finally, before reaching out and shaking her hand. "Welcome to Marlstone Hall."

"You're a very polite young lady," Rebecca pointed out.

"Mummy says we must be welcoming to everyone who comes here," Rose replied, before pulling her hand away. "It's never nice to be rude and we must make everyone feel at home. Some people come here from a very long way away."

"I'm sure they do," Rebecca said, still marveling at the girl's penchant for formality at such a young age. "And do you like living here in such an old house? There's lots of room to play in, isn't there?"

Rose thought for a moment, before nodding.

"And have you ever seen a ghost?" Jonathan called out.

Rebecca turned to him.

"What?" he continued. "I'm just getting to the important bit."

"My husband can be a little... direct," Rebecca said, turning to Rose again. "Sometimes he asks questions without stopping to think about how they might make people feel."

Rose opened her mouth to say something, but at the last second she held back. Turning, she looked over her shoulder as if she expected to see someone in the empty corridor, and then she looked up at Rebecca again. Finally, reaching into her pocket, she took out a rusty old brass key and – after a moment's further consideration – she reached out and pressed it into Rebecca's hand.

"You might need that," she whispered, before taking a step back. "I hope you don't, but you might. But don't tell Mummy that I gave it to you. She wouldn't like it if she knew."

"What is this key for?" Rebecca asked

cautiously, turning it around and seeing that it certainly seemed to be very old. "Is it for a door? A door to a room? What -"

"Please don't tell her," Rose said, suddenly turning and running out of the room.

"Well that was dramatic, wasn't it?" Jonathan mused, making his way over to join his wife. "How much extra pocket money do you think Rose gets for her performances? The creepy little girl thing is usually a winner, isn't it? Quite cliched, though. Then again, people don't usually like originality, do they? They *want* the cliches and all that crap."

He took the key from her hands and held it up, letting it glint in the light.

"This is starting to feel less like a haunted house and more like an escape room," he added with a smile. "I've got a feeling we'll have the whole think thoroughly debunked by the morning. If not much earlier."

Before she could finish, Rebecca saw Rose peering around a corner at the far end of the corridor. As soon as she realized that she'd been spotted, the girl pulled away and her footsteps could be heard racing off into the house. In that moment, Rebecca couldn't help but wonder how much of her interaction with Rose had been scripted and how much had been genuine. Somewhere deep in her gut, she couldn't shake the feeling that Rose was desperately trying – in her own strange way – to ask for help.

CHAPTER FIVE

"IT GETS COLD AT this time of year," Ida said as she turned the small metal wheel at the base of the radiator, causing the house's pipes to briefly groan. "Especially at night. Perhaps now you understand why I shut most of the place off for the winter. It's simply too expensive to keep it all warm."

"Tell me about it," Jonathan said, standing at the window and looking out at the night, although in truth he could see very little. "Our bloody bills have gone up so much over the past year."

"Thank you for dinner," Rebecca said as she stirred her coffee. "We weren't expecting to you to go to so much trouble."

"Cooking has always been one of my fortes," Ida replied. "In another life, I would have made quite a good chef. Even if I say so myself."

"But instead you've devoted yourself to the ancestral home?" Jonathan said as he turned to look at her. "That's quite a commitment, especially in this day and age. Didn't you ever consider turning your back on the place and selling up?"

"Of course," Ida replied, watching him from her position in front of the empty fireplace, "but I felt a strange sense of duty to my inheritance." She made a point of looking around the sitting room, which was decorated by yet more paintings of long-dead figures who'd once inhabited the house. "I suppose I thought it would be such a terrible waste to see Marlstone Hall go to the dogs. Someone has to fight to keep the old traditions alive, don't they?"

"Even by turning them into tourist traps?"

"One does what one has to do," she countered archly, turning to him. "One finds a way to keep going, just as one's forebears did. If only so that one can pass something on to the next generation."

At that moment Rose entered the room, carrying a tray of biscuits. She made her way to the table and set the tray down, and then she glanced briefly at Rebecca before making her way over to her mother.

"Darling, thank you," Ida said, tousling the hair on top of the girl's head for a moment. "It's getting late. Go upstairs and brush your teeth and I'll be along soon to settle you into bed. I'm sure everyone would like to retire nice and early. Say goodnight to our guests."

"Goodnight," Rose said obediently, turning to Jonathan, before looking at Rebecca again. "I hope you sleep well."

"Thank you," Rebecca replied, feeling slightly unnerved by the intensity of the young girl's gaze. "You too."

Rose stared back at her for perhaps a second – at most a second and a half – longer than might be considered normal, before turning and making her way out of the room.

"You must forgive my daughter," Ida said, having clearly picked up on the slightly strange atmosphere. "I fear that being raised here hasn't been easy for her, and sometimes she gets her social cues a little wrong. Nothing too bad, of course, but I've noticed that people notice. I want to assure you, though, that she's a very happy and contented girl and her school work is going well."

"Does she go to school near here?" Jonathan asked.

"I teach her myself," Ida explained. "I already explained that to your wife, I believe. I teach her here at the house so that I know exactly what she's learning. Unfortunately I don't drive, so getting her to the nearest village each morning would be almost impossible. I certainly can't afford to have her ferried there and back by taxi, but we've come to a solution that I think works extremely well. She simply learns everything she needs to learn right here at Marlstone Hall."

***

A fox cried out somewhere in the distance, sounding briefly like a scream, as Jonathan Pearson stood outside on the south-facing terrace and looked out at the darkness.

A moment later, hearing the patio doors squeaking open, he turned to see that Ida was making her way out to join him.

"It's beautiful, isn't it?" she said, stopping next to him and lighting a cigarette. "You don't mind if I smoke, do you?"

"Of course not," he replied. "And yes, you're right. You're very lucky to live in this part of the country. It must be so peaceful."

"It would be, without the... troubles," she admitted as the cigarette's light briefly illuminated her features.

"Troubles?" he asked.

"The reason you're here in the first place?" she reminded him.

"Oh, I see. The *troubles*. Is that what you call them?"

"I can't think of a better word," she said, turning and looking up at the dark facade of

Marlstone Hall. Only a handful of windows were in any way illuminated; the rest of the building stood in complete darkness. "I know I promised that I wouldn't go into too much detail, because I want you to go into this without being influenced by my stories, but I feel it would be remiss of me not to give you fair warning."

She took a long, slow drag on the cigarette.

"This place isn't for the faint-hearted," she added. "You're not the first people to come here full of confidence, determined to prove that there are no ghosts here. Martin simply oozed a sense of superiority, but it didn't last long. By the time he left, he was really rather ashen."

"Is that so?"

"You don't believe me."

"I believe in what I can prove," he replied. "My wife and I are academics. We're trained to take things a little slow and make sure that we don't make wild assumptions. One of our -"

"Yes, I think I know what you're getting at," she said, cutting him off. "There's no need for the speech about academic approaches to these things. I'm not an imbecile, Mr. Pearson, I fully understand that what I'm claiming is rather spectacular. If I turn out to be correct, the implication is that humanity's understanding of death itself is... rather flawed."

"That would be an understatement."

"So I get that you have a vested interest in

maintaining the status quo," she added as she took another puff on her cigarette.

"I wouldn't describe it quite like that."

"All I ask is that you approach the next few nights with an open mind," she continued. "I don't expect you to naively believe that there are ghosts here from the get-go, but can you at least allow for the possibility that there might be?"

"You're asking me to believe something extraordinary," he pointed out.

"I'm painfully aware of that fact."

She looked down at her cigarette for a few seconds.

"You have no idea how hard it is running this place as a single mother," she told him, and for the first time her tone of voice seemed to admit just the faintest hint of doubt. "I always assumed that I was simply going to assist my husband in his endeavors, but once he died..."

"Do you mind if I ask what happened?" Jonathan asked.

"His car was hit by a lorry about five miles from here," she explained. "He didn't stand a chance. I knew immediately that I had to continue his work, of course. The idea of abandoning everything, of letting Marlstone Hall fail, barely even entered my head. His family tried to stop me taking everything on, of course, but I stood firm and fortunately Henry had anticipated that there might be problems. He had a crack team of lawyers on standby, and his family ended up with nothing. Except resentment, that is. And that's another reason I have to make this place work. I want to stick a middle finger up at the whole lot of those sour-faced aristocrats."

"You have no contact with them at all?"

"It's just me and Rose against the world," she told him, before stubbing the cigarette out on the wall and tossing the butt onto the ground. "That's just the way the cookie has crumbled, but I've never been afraid of a challenge. And I might as well be honest with you, Mr. Pearson. I am very desperate for Marlstone Hall to turn out to be haunted, because at least then I have something to market to the tourists. Without a good ghost story, this place is just another pile of brick and stone."

She began to make her way back inside, before stopping just inside the patio doors and turning to him again.

"But don't let me influence you," she said softly. "I'm very confident that you'll find that there are ghosts here. And when you do, you'll have no choice. You'll simply *have* to admit that I'm right."

Once she was gone, Jonathan considered her words for a moment. He still had absolutely no belief whatsoever that ghosts might be real, but he could at least bring himself to admire Ida Sinclair's determination. And then, a moment later, he glanced up at the windows and saw a figure staring down at him.

Realizing that young Rose was watching, he smiled and offered a tentative wave. She, in turn, merely continued to observe him for a few more seconds before slowly stepping back into the shadows.

"Right," he said, taking a deep breath as he realized that the night air out on the terrace was getting a little too cold for his liking. "Time to get inside and do what Rebecca and I do best. Let's debunk the ghost stories here once and for all."

CHAPTER SIX

AN OWL HOOTED SOMEWHERE far off, beyond the windows of the room Ida had set up for the Pearsons.

"Four sevens," Jonathan said, setting down a seven of clubs on top of the three other sevens, then moving them all over to the used pile. "And a three."

Glancing at his watch, he saw that the time was now slightly after one in the morning. He and Rebecca had been playing endless rounds of Shithead for a couple of hours now, and he had to admit that his strength was flagging just a little. Still, as his wife placed two fives down, he knew that there was still a long way to go yet. Besides, she was something like 35-17 ahead, which remarkable for a supposed 'game of luck'.

"You can take a nap if you like," she told him, having evidently sensed his tiredness. "It only takes one of us to sit up. I'll wake you if anything happens."

"I don't want to miss the action," he said with a faint smile.

"Ha," she replied, watching as he set down an eight, then adding a ten of her own and turning the deck over. She then set down another three. "I don't think there's going to be much in the way of action tonight. Don't you think there's an overall air of such... sadness about this house? Of desperation?"

"Houses don't have airs of anything."

"You know what I mean."

"Actually, I don't," he told her. "I can't help thinking that you're reading too much into things."

He studied his cards for a moment.

"Ida Sinclair's certainly clinging on by her fingertips," he admitted as he set down a four.

"And she really thinks that a ghost story might save the place?"

He shrugged.

"I don't see how," she continued. "This just seems like one last desperate ruse while she waits to admit that the end is nigh. I'm sure someone could turn this place into a nice spa retreat or something like that, or a boutique hotel or some kind of -"

Before she could finish, they both heard a

door banging shut somewhere nearby, perhaps at the far end of the corridor outside the room.

"Hello," Jonathan said, setting his cards down before getting to his feet and heading to the door. "Sounds like we might have action. What are the odds that Mrs. Sinclair tries to generate some atmosphere? Perhaps the air of the house is about to get more interesting."

Opening the door, he leaned out and looked both ways along the corridor, but he saw nothing of note.

"Well?" Rebecca asked, standing and walking over to join him.

"It was probably just one of them going to the bathroom," he suggested. "People still do that, right? Even in haunted houses people have to get on with the mundane drudgery of life and -"

"Listen!" she hissed, suddenly holding up a hand.

He fell silent, and after a few seconds they both heard the sound of soft footsteps making their way along one of the nearby corridors.

Jonathan immediately turned to Rebecca, just as she stepped out into the corridor and looked toward the far end.

"Spooky," Jonathan whispered. "Someone -"

"It's a child," she said before he could finish.

"How can you tell?"

"It's obvious," she continued. "It's too quiet for an adult, especially for Ida Sinclair. I can just tell somehow."

"Then young Miss Rose must be up and about," he suggested.

"Maybe," she replied, listening as the footsteps moved further and further away, "but we wouldn't be doing our job properly if we didn't go and check, would we? At least... one of us should go. Perhaps you should stay here and wait in case there are any other strange noises."

"Suits me," he told her. "Good luck following the girl around. Give me a call if you spot a hideous poltergeist spewing ectoplasm, won't you? That might liven things up a bit."

***

Reaching the end of another corridor, Rebecca stopped again. She'd been following the sound of footsteps for a few minutes now, sometimes briefly getting a little closer but inevitably always losing them again. Now she was starting to wonder just where the child was going, since she felt fairly sure that there must have been several opportunities to slip into a bathroom by now.

Whereas the previous corridors had featured numerous doors, the corridor ahead appeared to have only one. Making her way closer, Rebecca realized that this particular door was markedly different to the rest; for one thing it looked much older, and for another it appeared to have been afforded very little care and attention over the years. Indeed, as she stopped in front of the door and reached out to touch its mottled surface, she couldn't help but notice that this poor door had quite clearly been neglected.

"You've haven't been looked after very much, have you?" she said under her breath as she felt the wood and realized that it felt very cold.

A moment later she heard the footsteps again, and this time she felt sure that they were coming from the other side of the door. She hesitated for a moment before trying the handle, and then – finding that the door was locked – she crouched down and peered through the somewhat dirty keyhole.

She saw a moonlit corridor beyond, with pale blue light shining from up high. After a few seconds, just as she blinked, she spotted a small shape moving from the shadows and heading around the far corner, and she realized that her early supposition had been correct. The 'shape' had most certainly been that of a child, and she felt fairly sure too that it had looked – in silhouette, at least – quite like young Rose.

Getting to her feet, she reached into her

pocket and fished out the key she'd been given by the girl earlier. The coincidence seemed too neat, unless it had been planned that way; she reached down and slid the key into the lock and it fitted perfectly, and then she gave it a turn. Although she felt some slight resistance, as if this particular lock perhaps hadn't been disturbed for a while, she was able to turn the key all the way and finally she heard a satisfying clicking sound, before finally she managed to pull the door open.

The hinges, naturally, emitted a groaning sound as if they too were quite unaccustomed to be asking to perform their one task in life.

Immediately feeling the cold air ahead, Rebecca stepped forward. She knew that technically she should go back and fetch Jonathan, but in that moment she wasn't quite in the mood to hear his endless stream of comments and she told herself that there was no harm in her simply checking out what appeared to be an abandoned part of the house. She wondered briefly whether she should call out, before reminding herself that there was no need to announce her arrival.

Besides, she felt fairly sure that she had been lured through the door in the first place. After all, why else would Rose have given her the key earlier?

After pulling the key out from the lock in case she needed it again later, she set off along the corridor. She couldn't help noticing that the air seemed to get colder with each step, and when she brushed a hand against the wooden paneling on the wall she noted that it was almost icy. The sound of her own footsteps seemed different here, somehow closer and louder, and as she reached the end of the corridor and looked around the corner she realized that she was moving away from the benefit of the moonlight.

The corridor ahead was entirely dark and chilly, with absolutely no natural light at all.

Spotting a switch on the wall, she gave it a quick flick, but she wasn't exactly surprised when she found that it did nothing. This part of the house had clearly been shuttered entirely for the winter, although she wondered whether it was wise – in the long term, at least – to let the place become so terribly cold.

Reaching into her pocket again, she quickly pulled out the flashlight that had become an essential part of her kit, and when she switched the narrow beam on she found herself looking along a rather bare and drab corridor.

The one truly noticeable aspect of this part of the house, she realized, was that the corridors were a little narrower and the ceilings were a little lower, and she couldn't help but wonder whether – in days gone by – these might have been the servants' quarters. Certainly no attempt had been made to make them even slightly as welcoming as the other areas. Then again, she supposed that only the tourist-friendly parts of the house were deemed worthy of attention these days.

Making her way forward, she noted that a couple of minutes had passed now since she'd last heard the footsteps. She still couldn't quite shake the sense that she'd been deliberately baited into this side of Marlstone Hall, and she couldn't help wondering whether Ida Sinclair and her daughter believed they could fool her with a little piece of theater.

As she approached the far end of the corridor, she was already starting to wonder whether someone was going to leap out from a hidden wardrobe, or whether perhaps some other attempt to scare her might arise. A few seconds later, however, she realized that she could hear floorboards creaking somewhere nearby and she saw that a bare wooden door had been left wide open.

"It's okay," she heard Rose's voice saying, sounding a little hushed now as if she was trying to not be heard. "You don't have to be scared. Someone's coming to help us."

CHAPTER SEVEN

THE DOOR'S HINGES CREAKED – rather predictably – as Rebecca pushed it open and found herself looking into a fairly small and barren room. There was no furniture at all, but enough moonlight was falling through the solitary window to make the flashlight unnecessary.

After flicking the switch on the flashlight's side, she saw that Rose was kneeling all alone on the floor, looking toward the far end of the room. A moment later the girl turned and looked over her shoulder, catching Rebecca's gaze.

"Hello," Rebecca said after a moment's silence. "What are you doing all the way through here? It's so cold."

She waited for Rose to say something, but the little girl merely looked down as if she felt guilty about the fact that she'd been found. That didn't quite line up with Rebecca's theory that the whole situation was a set-up, and a moment later Rose looked the other way, seemingly waiting for something else to happen.

"There's not a lot in here, is there?" Rebecca continued, stepping into the room and looking around. The most noticeable feature was a crack in the wall, running from the skirting board all the way up to the ceiling. Otherwise the room was empty, devoid even of any furniture. "Does this part of the house not get shown to visitors very much?"

A floorboard groaned very loudly beneath her left foot; indeed, she felt the board shift slightly, almost as if it might break at any moment.

Stopping next to Rose, she looked down and immediately saw fear in the girl's eyes. Unable to shake the sense that she was somehow intruding, that she'd interrupted something important, she once again looked around the room in the hope that she might spot something.

"Does your mother know that you're here?" she asked. "If -"

"Please don't tell her!" Rose blurted out.

Rebecca looked down at her again.

"Please," Rose continued, and now she seemed to be almost close to tears. After a moment she stumbled to her feet and grabbed Rebecca's hand, quickly squeezing her tight. "You mustn't tell her!"

"Alright, I won't tell her," Rebecca said cautiously, "but can you at least tell *me* what you're doing in here? Little girls aren't supposed to go climbing out of bed at all hours of the night. I thought I heard you talking to someone just now."

"I... was talking to them."

"Who?"

Rose hesitated, seemingly a little puzzled, before turning and looking toward the other end of the room.

"Them" she said again.

Once more following her gaze, Rebecca still saw no sign of anyone. Instead she found herself staring at more cracks on the walls, and while there were plenty of shadows she could already tell that there was certainly nobody hiding anywhere.

"Can't you see them?" Rose whispered.

"I'm afraid I don't know who or what I'm *supposed* to be seeing," Rebecca admitted.

Letting go of the older woman's hand, Rose took a step back.

"I thought you'd be able to," she said softly, with a sense of disappointment already filling her voice. "I just... I really thought it'd only by Mummy who couldn't. But I suppose that's why they can't make new friends very easily."

"What exactly are you talking about?" Rebecca asked. "Rose, it's alright, I'm on your side and you can tell me anything. There's no need to -"

"No!" Rose blurted out, suddenly stepping past her and holding up a hand. "Don't touch her!"

"Who are you talking to?" Rebecca asked.

"Just... don't touch her," Rose continued, speaking to a patch of thin air. "I don't know why, but I don't think you should. I must have got something wrong, but there's still time for me to work it out. I won't let you down, I promise, and the important thing is that Mummy doesn't know where you are. I just thought Mrs. Pearson might know more than Mr. Delaney did, that's all."

She glanced up at Rebecca, and then she turned to look at the empty space again.

"I'll work it out, I promise," she added finally. "Please don't be scared. I won't let anyone hurt you again and... I don't know how, but I'll find a new friend for you."

***

"So do you want to tell me what that was all about?" Rebecca asked a couple of minutes later, as she led Rose back along one of the cold corridors. "You really think you were talking to someone, don't you?"

She waited for an answer, but Rose had fallen very quiet now.

"It must get lonely living here," Rebecca

continued. "It's never nice to be lonely, no matter how old you are. I have a daughter who's only a year or two older than you, and sometimes I worry that she can be lonely sometimes. Do you have any friends?"

"Not really," Rose admitted.

"But you clearly have quite the imagination," Rebecca pointed out. "You know, I wouldn't blame you at all if you'd decided that you want to invent some friends so that you have someone to hang out with. Do you think there's a possibility that you've done that? Might your friends be imaginary?"

She shook her head.

"Then what are they?"

"They're people who lived here a long time ago," Rose explained cautiously, as if she herself didn't quite understand. "They died a long time ago too, and they've been here ever since. I don't think they want to be, though. They seem really sad but — please, you mustn't tell Mummy about them."

"Of course not," Rebecca said as they reached the old door, which she carefully opened, "but why are you so worried about that?"

"I don't know," Rose said cautiously, barely able to look her in the eye now. "I didn't want anyone to know about them. Not that they're really real."

"Are you sure about that?" Rebecca asked.

"You gave me a key to this door earlier. I can't help thinking that maybe on some level you wanted me to follow you. And I heard you saying out loud that someone had come to help them. You seemed quite pleased about the fact. Am I supposed to be that person?"

"I don't know," Rose said again.

"Do you mind if I come and take a look around in this part of the house tomorrow? I'll be able to see more in the daytime, but I'll only do it if you say that I can."

"What if Mummy asks why you're there?"

"I'll make up some kind of excuse. I'll say that it's totally random. Is that alright with you?"

Rose thought about that question for a moment before finally nodding, although she still seemed a little unconvinced.

"Now why don't you go to bed?" Rebecca continued, briefly touching the side of the girl's face. "You're so cold, Rose. And look, you're not even wearing anything on your feet. If you're going to go wandering around in the cold parts of the house, you really need to wrap up a little warmer. Do you understand?"

"Yes," Rose said, before stepping through the doorway and then turning to look at her again. "Thank you, Mrs. Pearson."

"Call me Rebecca."

"Thank you, Rebecca. And -"

In that moment she suddenly looked past her, as if something had caught her attention at the far end of the cold corridor. Turning, Rebecca looked through into the moonlit space but saw nothing, and a moment later she heard Rose's footsteps rushing away.

"Everything's going to be just fine!" she called after the girl, who'd already disappeared around the far corner and was evidently going back to her own bedroom.

Once she was alone, Rebecca turned and began to push the old door shut. At the last second, however, she stopped as she found herself looking once more along the cold corridor. She knew that she needed to remain calm and logical, indeed she'd spent much of her career trying to avoid letting emotion creep into her decision-making processes, yet for a few seconds she couldn't shake the feeling that somebody was in the corridor. Or, if they weren't actually *in* there, their presence most certainly seemed to be lingering. Looking at the far corner, she realized to her utmost surprise that she was actually surprised not to see anyone.

After pushing the door shut and locking it, she slipped the key back into her pocket and made her way along the corridor. She was already a little worried that she might be lost, but she supposed that she would be able to find Jonathan in the bedroom fairly quickly.

The old door, meanwhile, stood still and silent – just as it had stood still and silent for more than a century. Precious little had been done to refurbish it over the years. Multiple renovations and 'refreshments' had been carried out by various owners, but somehow the work had always managed to miss this particular door and the corridors to which it linked. Indeed, this could most certainly be said to remain the oldest untouched part of the house still standing.

And if anyone had happened to peer through the keyhole at that moment, looking into the cold part of the house, they would have immediately seen a cold dead eye staring straight back through.

CHAPTER EIGHT

THE FOLLOWING MORNING, HAVING eaten breakfast and then returned to the room so that she could prepare for the day, Rebecca Pearson stepped out onto the landing and immediately saw that her husband was examining some framed photographs on the far wall.

"Anything interesting?" she asked as she made her way over.

Nearby, rain was tapping against one of the windows as the weather outside continued to take a distinct turn for the worse.

"Maybe, maybe not," Jonathan replied noncommittally. "I was just looking at these. They appear to show images from the building's past."

"It looks very grand in that one," she pointed out, tapping at the glass in front of a small black-and-white photo. "They're all dressed up as if they're off on a jolly. When do you think this one was taken, Jonathan?"

"Oh, the 1920s or early 1930s, I'd say," he replied, peering more closely at the photo. "Judging by the styles in the image. My best guess would be about 1930 or 1931, which is when those styles had begun to reach our shores from the Americas. You can tell mainly from the dresses the women are wearing, it's a particular style that only began to be advertised in contemporary magazines around -"

Suddenly realizing that Rebecca wasn't paying a great deal of attention, he turned to see that she was instead peering at a smaller photo next to the door. Shuffling over, he took a look too and found himself peering at an image of half a dozen young boys and girls standing outside the front of the building.

"Evacuees," he said, with a trace of sadness in his voice. "I can't imagine how terrifying it must have been for them to be uprooted from their homes, taken away from their families and shipped off to live with complete strangers. I know it was all for their own good, to keep them safe from falling bombs during the war, but still... can you imagine if we had to suddenly send Alicia away to stay with people we'd never met?"

His voice trailed off for a moment.

"They were brave little souls," he added

finally. "You can see the fear in their eyes, can't you? They had no idea whether their homes would still be there, even if the war ended in their favor."

"Bravery has nothing to do with it."

Startled, they both turned to see that Ida had made her way through to the hallway and was watching them from the doorway. Already, both Rebecca and Jonathan had noted her ability to suddenly show up in various parts of the house without first announcing her arrival.

"They had no decisions to make," she continued. "They were children, they merely did as they were told. I don't see where bravery comes into it."

"Bravery takes many different forms, I suppose," Jonathan suggested.

"In their cases, they might have been better staying at home and risking the bombs," Ida explained. "The six young children in that photograph all died here. A rather nasty outbreak of typhus struck shortly after they arrived in late 1939. The deaths could perhaps have been avoided, but the correct treatment wasn't available for them at the time. Or, rather, it wasn't correctly administered."

"That's awful," Rebecca replied. "I had no idea that the history of the house contained so much tragedy."

"It's an old house," Ida pointed out. "Old

houses tend to have had bad things happen in them. Tragedy accumulates like dust. Bad things happen *anywhere*, if you wait long enough. Why, I bet there's not one square foot of land anywhere in the country where something truly awful didn't once happen. I'm amazed that we're not absolutely swimming in a seething mass of ghostly presences."

"Do you think the ghost stories here at Marlstone Hall have something to do with these boys?" Rebecca asked.

"I wasn't going to tell you too much about that," she continued, "because I didn't want to influence you, but..." She paused for a moment, before taking a step forward. "I suppose there's one part of the tour that I might bring up for your benefit. Just to point you in the right direction, I suppose."

***

"The old smoking room," she said a few minutes later, having led them through into a high-ceilinged room toward the southern end of the property. "In days gone by, after dinner the men would retire here to smoke and discuss important matters while the women... well, I suppose they would go elsewhere and discuss flowers and sewing."

"It's cold in here," Rebecca observed, stepping forward and looking around at the mostly bare walls.

Heading over to the far side, she saw a display showing some young boys sitting in makeshift beds.

"Many years ago," Ida continued, "when the children became sick, they were isolated in this very room. One by one, they were brought here by a well-meaning nurse and... attempts were made to treat them. Those attempts didn't go very well, however."

Looking at one particular photo, Rebecca saw a painfully thin boy standing next to a window. He was leaning against a crutch, as if he was too weak to support himself.

Turning to her left, she saw the same window now – almost a century had passed since that boy had stood in that exact spot. When she turned to study his image again, she was struck by his gaunt features and by the dark shadows under his eyes, almost as if death had already set one hand on his shoulders and he was waiting for the final moment.

"It's not a pleasant way to go, by all accounts," Ida explained. "Cardiac failure is often the immediate cause, but there are many contributing factors including pneumonia and delirium. My research suggests that the nurse who tried to treat them was a good woman, but that she was simply in over her head. Some of the actions made the situation actively worse. She even encouraged the sick children to mingle with the healthy for a while, and of course that only made sure that they all ended up becoming ill. By the time she realized that she needed to get help, it was too late. That's what the local doctor claimed, at least."

Jonathan walked over to join Rebecca in front of the display.

"When treated," Ida added, "typhus can often be overcome. When untreated, or treated incorrectly, the death rate can be well over fifty per cent. In this case it was worse. After the tragedy, the authorities made the no doubt wise decision to not send any more evacuees to Marlstone Hall. I'm not sure that anyone would have argued with that choice too much."

"So," Jonathan said, turning to her, "I suppose this is part of your ghost story, is it? You believe that the ghosts of some or all of these children are still haunting the house to this day."

"I didn't say that."

"But you believe it," he continued. "You wouldn't have gone to all this trouble to print up these displays otherwise. Besides, ghostly young boys and girls would no doubt tug on the heartstrings of your visitors. There's nothing quite so terrifying as the prospect of bumping into a spectral young chap in your bedroom one night, is there?"

"That's a rather cynical way of looking at things," she suggested.

"In my line of work, cynicism is often merited," he replied. "And in yours, it's no doubt rather profitable."

"I'm going to let you look around the house some more," she told him, clearly untroubled by his attitude. "Again, I want you to come to your own conclusions, and I certainly don't want you to be able to claim that I have tried to guide you in a certain direction. I would merely like to point out that *you're* the ones talking about the ghosts of those children. I have merely informed you of the house's history and you've run with the rest. There's even a small memorial to the dead children outside. If you're interested, it's well sign-posted."

She turned and began to make her way out of the room.

"I shall see you for lunch at one o'clock," she called back to them both. "Until then, please feel free to explore the house at your leisure."

"Can you believe that?" Jonathan chuckled, turning to his wife. "Ghostly children. It's about as cliched as you can get. The woman clearly has no shame."

He waited for her to reply, but after a moment he realized that she seemed to be almost transfixed by the photo.

"Rebecca?"

"Hmm?" Turning to him, she was clearly in a world of her own. "I'm sorry," she continued, "I was just thinking about the children."

"And that's how she gets people," he said, raising one eyebrow. "It's breathtaking, really. She's using the deaths of those youngsters for financial gain. For profit. Or at least she's trying to, although mercifully she doesn't seem to be doing very well at it. She's lucky someone doesn't report her for violating child labor laws."

"I don't think those laws apply to *dead* children," Rebecca pointed out.

"That still doesn't mean that it sits well with me," he muttered, before glancing at the window and seeing that the rain outside was falling a little harder now. "She mentioned a memorial. I know you said you wanted to take a more detailed look around the house, but I think I'm going to check that memorial out. I want to see exactly how far Ida Sinclair is willing to go in her attempt to cultivate her little ghost story."

CHAPTER NINE

RAIN WAS BATTERING THE glass panels of the conservatory as Rebecca stepped through and spotted Rose sitting with a book by the window.

As soon as she realized that she'd been seen, the young girl closed the book.

"It's alright," Rebecca said, making her way over and stopping for a moment to look out at the increasingly terrible weather that was drenching the lawn and battering the distant trees. "It's not a very nice day out there, is it? I don't blame you for wanting to curl up with a good book."

She waited for an answer, but once again there was something strangely withdrawn about Rose, as if she was in a perpetual state of guilt – or perhaps even shame.

"Don't worry," Rebecca continued, sitting

opposite her, "I haven't told your mother about our meet-up during the night. That can remain our little secret."

"Can you help ghosts?" Rose asked.

"What exactly do you mean by *help*?"

"If they're... trapped," Rose continued cautiously. "If they're somewhere they don't want to be. Or if they're lonely. Can you help them to leave?"

"Well, I think I'd need to know exactly why you're asking me that question. Do you think that there are some ghosts trapped here at Marlstone Hall?"

She waited, but Rose seemed too nervous to reply.

"Have *you* seen any ghosts here, Rose?"

At this, Rose immediately looked over at the doorway, as if she was worried that her mother might arrive at any moment. For a moment she merely sat in silence; the only sound came from more and more rain pattering against the nearby windowpanes.

"You can tell me," Rebecca continued. "Don't worry, I'm not going to bite. I just want to know whether you think you've seen any ghosts here at the house. I know, for example, that your mother sometimes talks about some young boys and girls who might be here. They were probably about your age when they arrived at the house. Does that ring any bells for you?"

"I don't know," Rose said cautiously, although she was clearly holding something back.

The silence continued for several more seconds, stretching out and becoming louder still. In that space of time, the rain already sounded slightly stronger and more insistent.

"Are you scared of something?" Rebecca asked, feeling as if she was getting closer to the crux of the matter – but also that the final little push required both tact and patience.

"I'm scared she might find them," Rose said finally.

"Who?" Rebecca replied.

"The nurse," Rose added, and now there were tears in her eyes. "The nurse who killed them after they came here. She's been looking for them ever since and... I'm really scared she's going to find them soon. At least... that's what Mummy thinks."

"Right," Rebecca said cautiously, starting to worry that all this talk of ghosts was having a very negative impact on the girl's state of mind. "I think it's important to remember that ghosts aren't actually real." She waited for a reply, but she couldn't help wondering whether Rose's mother had been filling the girl with all sorts of crazy claims. "You really don't need to let yourself be scared of shadows and bumps in the night."

"But the nurse..."

Rose's voice trailed off for a seconds, before she slowly looked past Rebecca as if she still expected to see someone else entering the room.

"She's been looking for them for so long," she added finally, as more fear entered her voice. "When she finds them, I think she wants to punish them for making her seem like a bad person."

***

Although the umbrella afforded him a degree of protection from the rain, Jonathan still found – as he carefully stepped around larger puddles in the unevenly paved rockery – that he was getting quite wet.

Having made his way around to the far end of the garden, he'd finally reached the small memorial to the six children who'd died at the house during the Second World War. This memorial took the form of a gathering of rocks, arranged to form a mound rising approximately three or four feet up from the ground, while the names of the children had been carefully etched into a stone placed on one side.

Crouching down, with rain loudly battering his umbrella, Jonathan had to squint in an attempt to read the names properly.

"Jonathan Wheaton," he read out loud, "Douglas Croft, Winifred Jones, Ernest

Micklemore, Caroline Day, Meredith Pool."

He let those names hang in the damp, cold air for a moment. He'd never heard of Marlstone Hall before the dinner party a few weeks earlier, and he'd certainly never heard the tragic tale of the six evacuees who'd died of typhus. Part of him was still puzzled that the children couldn't have been saved; even in the late 1930s, treatment for typhus should have been available and while one death seemed plausible, the fact that all six had succumbed felt... wrong, somehow.

"Rest in peace," he muttered, standing up again and looking around, before spotting some piles of soil that had been left nearby.

Not wanting to get his shoes filthy in the mud, he only dared to venture as far as the edge of the rocks, but now he could see that the garden in this area had been significantly disturbed. In fact, the place was a complete mess, with old wooden slats have been tossed aside and sections of a wire fence left partially wound up on their sides. The constant deafening hammering of rain made it somewhat difficult for him to even think straight, but for a moment he found himself wondering just how far Ida Sinclair might go in order to promote her little ghost stories.

Spotting a shape that had been discarded near his feet, he reached down and picked up couple of pieces of stone. After turning them around for a moment he was able to slot them more or less together, and he realized that he was holding two pieces of a broken stone cross.

Turning, he saw a damaged stump on the top of the memorial. When he reached up and tried to fit the broken cross in that spot, he found that it slid into place perfectly. Evidently someone had at some point damaged the cross. Indeed, now that he looked more closely at the memorial, he realized that several parts had been chipped away, and he was starting to wonder whether it might have been subjected to some kind of attack.

Spotting an abandoned shovel nearby, he was already trying to fit the pieces of this particular mystery together and he couldn't help but imagine Ida Sinclair slamming the shovel's tip against the memorial in an attempt to break it apart. He had no idea why she – or anyone – would do such a thing, especially since he supposed that the memorial might make a decent centerpiece for the visitor experience, but he couldn't ignore the chunks that had been broken away from various spots on the stone.

And then, glancing at the main house, he froze as he realized that he could see a face at one of the windows.

Although rain was beating down against the grass, creating a haze that made it slightly more difficult to see properly, he squinted as he stared at the face. Standing at one of the higher windows, this face – which appeared to be that of a young boy – was simply watching him, and after a moment Jonathan saw a second small figure stepping into view.

A moment after that two more children appeared at another window, swiftly followed by another pair.

"Now that's a rather nifty little trick," he whispered, and his brain was already whirring as he tried to work out exactly how the effect was being achieved.

Animatronics?

Projection?

Actors in old-fashioned clothing?

Assuming that Ida Sinclair didn't have a small troupe of child actors stashed away somewhere inside Marlstone Hall, Jonathan quickly told himself that most likely he was witnessing some kind of projection. He looked at the patio doors and then began to count along and up, trying to work out exactly which room the figures appeared to be in. When he looked up at the windows again, however, he saw that five of the figures had now vanished.

Only one child remained, and even from a distance of forty or fifty feet Jonathan felt that he could make out dark shadows under the figure's eyes. He couldn't be sure, but he was starting to think that the figure was a young boy, although further conjecture was stifled as the figure slowly stepped back and disappeared from view.

Left standing alone in the rain, beneath his umbrella, Jonathan kept his gaze fixed on the windows in the hope that the figures might return. After a few seconds, realizing that the little performance appeared to be over for now, he took one last look at the damaged memorial before starting to pick his way back over the rocks, heading toward the house.

"All we have to do is find your little projection equipment, Mrs. Sinclair," he muttered under his breath, slightly annoyed now as he felt cold rainwater seeping into his shoes, "and then we'll have you very much banged to rights."

CHAPTER TEN

"EMMA KEMP," REBECCA SAID, standing in one of the old bedrooms upstairs and looking at a large display showing a photograph of a woman in an old-fashioned nursing uniform. "So this was the woman who was supposed to look after the children when they arrived at Marlstone Hall?"

Stepping closer, she saw the woman's smiling face. The photograph had been massively enlarged, leaving the resolution rather poor, but Rebecca could still see that she had a seemingly friendly countenance. Sitting on a chair with her hands on her lap, the nurse certainly didn't appear to be some malevolent or incompetent monster; then again, Rebecca knew that it was far too soon to judge this particular book by its cover.

Scanning the text on the display, she quickly

picked up the basics. Emma Kemp had been fairly new to the nursing profession when the war had broken out, and she'd been sent to Marlstone Hall when the plan had been to have a large number of evacuees at the property. Perhaps, the display suggested, she'd been in a little too deep, thrust into a position for which she was ill-prepared. Following the deaths of the first six children, however, the plans for Marlstone Hall had been scrapped and Emma's career had been left in ruins. Rebecca couldn't help but feel sorry for the woman, and she felt sure that the psychological burden of so much guilt – whether or not it had been strictly deserved – must have been unbearable.

Hearing a floorboard creaking, she turned to see that Rose had barely dared to even step into the room.

"It's okay," she said with a smile, holding a hand out toward the girl. "There's nothing to be frightened of in here."

Rose looked around for a moment before finally edging forward.

"This was Ms. Kemp's bedroom, according to the information on the board," Rebecca continued. "Your mother seems to have gone to great lengths to research and document almost every element of the house's history."

Still looking around, Rose seemed a little paler than before.

"Let me ask you an important question," Rebecca continued, making her way over and taking the girl by the hand, then turning to look once more at the photograph of the nurse. "I want you to think carefully before you answer. Have you ever *actually* seen this woman in the house? I don't mean little fears or possible half glances, and I certainly don't mean bumps in the night. What I mean is... have you ever properly seen her anywhere apart from in photographs?"

"No," Rose said cautiously, "but -"

"And has anyone else ever claimed to have seen her?"

"I don't know," Rose replied, "but... Mummy says she saw her a few times."

"I'm sure she does," Rebecca said, rolling her eyes.

"Mummy says the nurse is looking for the children because she's mad at them."

"For what? For dying?"

"Mummy says everyone blamed the nurse when they died, and she got really sad and..."

Her voice trailed off for a moment, and then slowly she looked up. Following her gaze, Rebecca looked at the ceiling and saw a solitary wooden rafter running from one wall to the other.

"Mummy says she hung herself from a rope in here," Rose continued, "because she couldn't handle the guilt from what had happened. She did it right after the funeral. And ever since, people have heard scary noises coming from this part of the house, and some people have even seen the nurse hanging from up there, and sometimes she's down on the floor and she's walking around and she's trying to find the children because she's so angry and sad and -"

Running out of breath, she let out a gasp.

"It's quite alright," Rebecca said firmly, squeezing her hand a little tighter. "You're clearly a very imaginative young lady, but unfortunately your imagination has been fueled by lots of... well, by stories that aren't necessarily true. It's almost as if -"

Suddenly a loud bump rang out, and Rose instinctively scurried around until she could hide behind Rebecca. In turn, Rebecca looked toward the open doorway as she heard footsteps approaching, and finally she saw Ida Sinclair stepping into view.

"There you both are," Ida said with a smile as she stopped in the doorway. "I was starting to wonder where you could have gone. It's not as if the weather's very nice out there, is it? Is anyone interested in a light lunch in the next hour or so?"

"That sounds great," Rebecca said cautiously. "Actually, I'd also like to talk to you about something. Something very important." As those words left her lips, she realized that she could feel Rose's hand shaking with fear. "Mrs. Sinclair, it's about your daughter."

***

"Right, let's see here," Jonathan muttered, pushing open another door and stepping into yet another large, empty room up on the top floor of the house. "If I'm right..."

He stopped to look around for a moment before heading to the window. He could see the memorial in the distance, out in the rain-lashed garden, and already he felt certain that he'd counted correctly. He looked at the next window along, and in that instant he felt with absolute certainty that he'd found the exact spot where the six ghostly children had been standing.

Or, rather, where they'd *appeared* to be standing.

Crouching down, he looked more carefully at the glass, and now he realized that he could just about make out the remains of a small hand print.

"You're a stickler for details, Mrs. Sinclair," he said under his breath, as he saw that already the hand print was fading from the window's surface. "And timing too. Credit where it's due."

Turning, he looked around the room. Any furniture that had once been present was long since gone. All he saw were bare floorboards and bare walls. In truth, there was nothing particularly menacing about this space; he felt no shiver in his bones, no sense of being watched. At the same time, he also saw no sign of any projection equipment, even when he turned and looked up at the ceiling.

"Where are you?" he whispered, convinced that this must be the most likely explanation for the sight of the children.

Pacing around the room, he tried to find any hint of a hiding space, any crack in the wall that might be large enough to permit a projector to do its work. Reaching the window again, he realized that he was rather stumped. He still felt sure that a projector was by far the most likely means by which the image of the children might have been achieved, although now he was starting to return to some of the other possibilities.

The idea that six young actors were hidden away seemed utterly implausible, yet he couldn't shake the feeling that Mrs. Sinclair was willing to go to great lengths in her bid to make Marlstone Hall seem haunted.

And then, looking at the window again, he saw what appeared to be fresh hand prints in several spots on the glass. He felt sure that they hadn't been there just a minute or two earlier, and indeed they were already fading again. He also knew for a fact that nobody could have crept into the room and put them there without being noticed, so now he found himself considering another – albeit rather unusual – possibility.

"Magic glass," he said out loud, before touching the pane and trying to find anything unusual. "Or... some kind of screen built into the damn thing."

Although he wasn't entirely sure what he meant by that suggestion, he was starting to wonder whether Ida Sinclair might have found some kind of new high-tech glass that was capable of producing images without any need for a projector. He wasn't entirely up to date with the state of modern technology, but he found himself considering the possibility that she might have got her hands on a new-fangled device from Japan or some other country where such things often seemed to be developed first.

"I bet that's it," he said, and now he started searching for a power supply, although he figured that the window might be battery powered or even that a cord had been hidden inside the wall. "This is some next-level trickery."

Finally he realized that while his theory still had legs, there was no way to prove it without literally ripping the window from its frame. Even if the window's technology had been hidden away, however, he felt sure that there had to be *some* way of catching the trickery in action. Finally he told himself that if Ida Sinclair was smart, then he simply had to be a little smarter. No matter how much effort Ida had put into her little haunted house set-up, he believed – no, he *knew* – that he was ahead of the game and that sooner or later she was going to trip up.

"You're not going to get one over on me," he said firmly. "You might have tricked Martin Delaney, but even the greatest minds have their weak spots. Not me, though. And I'm going to particularly enjoy ruining your plans."

CHAPTER ELEVEN

"I'M SORRY," IDA SAID, bristling slightly as she carried another plate from the fridge and set it down onto the kitchen counter. "Mrs. Pearson, I'm really not sure that I like your tone."

"I'm sorry too, but I really think you need to think of your daughter," Rebecca replied. "It's clear to me already that she's living in fear in this house. I understand that you want to cultivate this... ghost story here at Marlstone Hall, but you can't do that at the expense of your daughter's upbringing."

"Cultivate a ghost story?" Ida said, taking the foil off a platter of cheese and meat, then turning to her. "Is that really what you think I'm doing here? Believe me, Mrs. Pearson, at first I tried extremely hard to ignore the entire situation."

"I get it," Rebecca continued. "It must be so

hard trying to make this place work, and in many ways I admire you for your efforts. But there has to be a limit. Just from talking to Rose a little this morning, I can tell that she's terrified. She believes these stories you've been coming up with, she's taking them to heart and at her young age she's still so impressionable. Perhaps it's difficult for you to see these things, but for someone entering your home environment for the first time the problem is quite pronounced."

"I see," Ida murmured, clearly momentarily troubled by what she was hearing. "So you think that I would prioritize financial considerations over my own daughter's well-being?"

"That's not what I said."

"But it's what you're implying," Ida pointed out. "You're right that Rose is a sensitive young thing, but doesn't that just prove that I'm right? I'm fully aware that she's picking up on certain... impressions here in the house. Hell, sometimes I've found that she senses impressions that I don't. You might think that I'm capable of making these things up, but do you really think that my daughter is so manipulative?"

"That's not what I'm saying at all," Rebecca replied with a heavy sigh.

"I've seen the ghost," Ida continued, before shaking her head. "There, I've admitted it. I was going to stay silent on that matter so that you could come to your own conclusions, but the truth is that I've seen the ghost of Emma Kemp with my own two eyes. It's happened twice, actually. The first time I was outside one afternoon and I happened to spot her at one of the windows. The second time I was woken in the night by the most almighty clattering sound, and when I went into the cold side of the house I saw her walking right past the end of a corridor. She even looked at me as she disappeared from sight."

"Is that right?" Rebecca asked, clearly unimpressed by the tale.

"Emma Kemp was accused of gross negligence following the deaths of those children," Ida explained. "I'm afraid I don't know whether the charge was merited or whether she was made a scapegoat, but either way she ended up hanging herself in her room. And ever since, her ghostly form has been seen searching the house, trying to find the ghosts of those children. If you don't believe me, you can read the half dozen accounts I've managed to locate over the years from other people who've encountered her."

Rebecca sighed.

"Of course you think I'm lying my face off," Ida added, "and that's fine, but I'd like to remind you that you *claim* to keep an open mind." She paused, before sliding the platter across the counter. "As for my daughter, I'm more than capable of taking care of her, thank you very much. I didn't invite you here to analyze my parenting skills, I invited you here to investigate the ghostly presence. I'd really prefer it if you would stay in your lane."

***

"I don't like this," Rebecca said once she'd found Jonathan, who was changing his rain-soaked socks in the bedroom. "I don't like it at all. Ida Sinclair can do whatever she damn well likes with her house, and with her own life too, but when the well-being of a child is at stake..."

She watched as her husband pulled a fresh pair of socks from the suitcase.

"Why are you wet?" she asked suddenly.

"Why indeed?" he murmured. "I went to check out the memorial, remember?"

"Of course. You mentioned something about that."

"Someone's been at it with a shovel," he continued. "What do you make of that, huh? The little cross on the top has been completely broken away. Why would someone physically attack a memorial to six dead children?"

"I have no idea," she told him.

"Ida Sinclair is a lot smarter than she looks," he explained. "I have to admit that I didn't have her figured out, not at first. I thought she was just another fool trying to dress up a bunch of silly stories, but now I'm starting to think that behind that demure appearance there's an extremely calculating mind."

"I agree with you," she admitted. "She's even willing to screw her own child's mental health over, just to maintain this entire fiction about a haunting. You don't think we should call someone, do you? Should we try to get social services involved?"

"I'm not sure they'd consider it to be a priority case," he pointed out.

"Rose Sinclair is really suffering," Rebecca insisted. "I don't think the profoundly damaging implications of this situation should be ignored. The girl is, what, eight years old? Something like that? She's at a crucial formative age and any damage that's done now might impact her development. She needs to grow up in a safe and nurturing environment, not in a home where she's constantly terrified."

"Kids are stronger than you think."

"Is that your answer?" she replied with a sigh. "You just want to trust her to get on with it?"

"Our hands are tied," he said as he got to his feet and stepped over to her. He took a moment to put his hands on the sides of her arms. "Rebecca, you're a wonderful mother and Alicia is so lucky to have you. Rose Sinclair, meanwhile, is really nothing to do with us. Social services certainly aren't going to come rushing out based on a report filed by two people rambling about ghosts. They've got far more serious cases to be dealing with, and they're already under-resourced as it is. The best thing we can do for young Rose is to resolve this situation by proving that her mother's claims are nonsense. Then perhaps they can both move on."

"I just hate seeing anyone so miserable," Rebecca said softly.

"I've got some equipment in the car that might be useful," he told her. "It detects wires and cables in walls, which I think might be how Ida is achieving some of her tricks. I'm going to go and grab it, and if it works as well as I think it might, we could have this whole thing figured out by evening. We might not even have to stay another night."

"And then what? We just sail off into the sunset and leave Rose behind?"

"I don't see what other options we have," he replied, kissing her on the cheek before heading across the room and slipping his shoes on. "You can't save the whole world. I've told you that many times. And sure, Rose might get a little screwed up by her childhood, but she'll hardly be alone in that. Not every kid can have a perfect family life like Alicia."

Opening the door, he stepped out into the corridor and then turned to his wife again.

"Are you coming?" he asked.

"I want to poke around a little more in the cold side of the place," she told him. "For whatever reason, that seems to be where most of the supposed paranormal activity is focused. I've got a feeling that Ida wants us to 'discover' that for ourselves, but I also think that Rose gave me that key for a very different reason. Rightly or wrongly, Rose genuinely seems to think that we can help and I want to figure out why. She was talking to someone last night, or at least she thought she was."

"Just don't get too involved," he said firmly. "I know what you're like, Rebecca. You're a sucker for a bleeding heart, and while that's a wonderful quality, you mustn't let it get in the way of our work here."

Once her husband was gone, Rebecca made her way to the window and looked out at the falling rain. She knew deep down that Rose Sinclair was really suffering, but she also knew that her husband had been broadly correct when he'd claimed that there was little they could do to help. At the same time, she worried that Ida Sinclair was far too invested in the ghost stories at Marlstone Hall to ever back down.

When push came to shove, would Ida abandon her foolish games – or would she instead abandon reality and logic entirely?

CHAPTER TWELVE

"I KNOW WHAT YOU'RE like, Rebecca," she muttered under her breath as she made her way along another corridor in the cold part of the house. "You're a sucker for a bleeding heart, Rebecca. You just feel too damn sorry for mistreated children, Rebecca."

Stopping at yet another doorway and looking into yet another empty room, she couldn't help but hear her husband's words going round and round in her thoughts.

"I just don't like it when adults pass their screw-ups directly to their kids," she added quietly. "It's hard enough for them growing up anyway, without -"

Suddenly hearing a distinct clanging sound – as if somebody had banged metal against metal –

she turned and looked ahead. The far end of the corridor showed no sign of movement, yet Rebecca felt sure that the sound meant somebody was nearby. She waited, and sure enough after a few more seconds she heard a faint shuffling noise, as if someone was trying to walk very quietly.

"Hello?" she called out.

Again she waited, before heading to the end of the corridor and looking around the corner. The air was so cold that she could see her own breath, but there was still no hint of another presence.

"Hello, is anyone here?" she continued, determined to confront the situation properly instead of pussyfooting around. "My name is..."

She hesitated as she realized that anyone else in the house would already know her name only too well.

"It's me," she said as she began to make her way along the corridor. "Rose, is that you? Mrs. Sinclair?"

Still making her way forward, she felt more determined than ever to get to the truth.

"I know that somebody's here," she explained, "so it would be better for all of us if you just come out. Rose, if it's you, nobody's going to be angry at you. And Mrs. Sinclair, if you're here, I hope you'll respect me enough to stop lurking in the shadows."

Reaching the end of the next corridor, she

looked around but saw only a series of closed doors. She tried the nearest handle, but when she pushed the door open she found herself merely looking into yet another of the house's interminable empty rooms. This entire wing of the house had clearly been stripped bare, and the room – with its exposed floorboards and cracks on the walls – was a far cry from the carefully cultivated grandeur of the rest of the place. Evidently Ida Sinclair had been telling the truth when she'd said that she could only afford to maintain and heat a small part of the building. The rest of Marlstone Hall had clearly been left to rot.

A moment later, hearing another clanging sound, Rebecca immediately turned and hurried along the corridor, determined to this time catch the culprit in the act. Already she could tell that the sound had seemed to come from right around the corner.

"Mrs. Sinclair," she said firmly, convinced now that this was who she was about to find, "if -"

As soon as she rounded the corner, she stopped as she saw that there was nobody in front of her. A sense of frustration was growing in her chest now – and she couldn't help but imagine Ida Sinclair hiding and giggling away to herself, playing yet another foolish prank in an attempt to create an unnerving atmosphere.

Forcing herself to stay calm, Rebecca tried to focus on more important matters. She listened to the silence of this part of the house for a moment longer, and then she began to slowly make her way forward, determined this time to maintain the advantage of surprise. Wherever Ida Sinclair might be lurking, there had to be a way to lure her out and expose her games.

***

Half an hour later, having stopped once more in one of the many empty rooms, Rebecca looked down at her watch. She'd decided to hide herself away in the hope that she might fool Ida into believing that she'd left altogether. Now, however, she was starting to wonder whether her plan might have backfired slightly.

As she once again saw her own breath in the air, Rebecca couldn't help but feel that she'd been sent running around in circles. Marlstone Hall was large – large enough for a person to get lost in – and while she didn't quite consider herself to be lost just yet, she reasoned that a person who knew the full layout would have a distinct advantage. She couldn't help glancing around, worried that somehow Ida might be observing her, although she spotted no obvious place where a small camera might have been hidden.

Stepping over to the window, she looked out and saw the memorial in the distance. In that moment her husband's words returned to her thoughts.

"I went to check out the memorial, remember?" he'd told her earlier. "Someone's been at it with a shovel. What do you make of that, huh? The little cross on the top had been completely broken away. Why would someone physically attack a memorial to six dead children?"

The memorial certainly seemed like something that would play a key role in any visit to the property, so Rebecca couldn't understand why Ida Sinclair would ever be responsible for such vandalism.

And then, just as she was starting to ponder that question a little more, she heard footsteps somewhere in one of the nearby corridors. Turning, she looked over her shoulder and listened as the footsteps moved away slightly, and then she made her way as quietly as possible to the door and looked out. She saw no sign of anyone – she hadn't really expected to, not now that she was getting used to the vagaries of the house – but she could still hear the footsteps, as if somebody was very calmly walking through this part of the building.

Hoping that perhaps Ida Sinclair had been tricked into thinking she was alone, Rebecca set off after those footsteps, while taking great care to remain as silent as possible.

For the next few minutes she found that she

was able to follow the footsteps quite easily. Although at each corner she saw no sign of anyone in the next corridor, she told herself that at least she was managing to keep up. Finally she reached yet another corner, and this time when she looked into the next corridor she heard a creaking sound just as she saw a door slowly swinging in its frame.

Whoever she was following, they had evidently passed this way just a few seconds earlier.

Determined to seize upon her opportunity, Rebecca began to walk quickly along the next corridor, heading straight for the door at the far end. She hurried her pace a little more, hoping that she might be about to finally catch Mrs. Sinclair, but when she stepped into the next room she found that it was once again empty.

Or at least, *almost* empty.

At the far end of the room, a large and somewhat dusty mirror had been left hanging on the wall. Stepping further into the space, Rebecca looked around and saw another door leading off into some other part of the house. She walked over and tried the handle, but she quickly found that this particular door remained locked. A few seconds later, hearing a faint scratching sound from the door's other side, she crouched down and tried to peer through the keyhole.

Squinting slightly, she was just about able to make out a patch of light on a wall in the next room, although so far the space appeared to be yet another of the seemingly endless empty shells in this part of the house. As the scratching sound continued, however, she realized that someone certainly seemed to be on the other side of the door, and she couldn't help but wonder whether this was another part of Ida Sinclair's theatrical attempt to construct a ghost story.

"Hello?" she said cautiously, keen to get the foolishness over with. "Mrs. Sinclair, are you there? It's Rebecca Pearson and I -"

Before she could finish, she heard a rustling sound and she looked down just in time to see a scrap of paper sliding under the door.

Picking the paper up, she turned it around and found that it was a roughly triangular piece that appeared to have been torn from a much larger page. The paper itself was yellowing and clearly quite old, and some almost indecipherable handwriting could just about be made out starting in one corner. Although she spent a moment trying to work out what the handwriting might say, she quickly understood that the task was hopeless. When she turned the paper over again, however, she saw two letters printed in fading black ink:

RA

After pondering the possible meaning of

those letters, she wondered whether the piece of paper was intended as some kind of clue in a game. She certainly wasn't in the mood for any of Ida Sinclair's silliness, and a moment later she looked at the keyhole again as she realized that the scratching sound had come to a stop.

Taking the key from her pocket – the same key that Rose had given her – she quickly tried it in this door too. She hadn't expected it to work, and of course it didn't, but she figured that the attempt had been worthwhile.

"What is this supposed to mean?" she asked out loud, looking at the scrap of paper again before getting to her feet and looking around the room.

She spotted her own reflection in the dirty mirror, and then she looked at the door again.

"I'm not in the mood to play games, Mrs. Sinclair," she continued. "This sort of thing might amuse certain types of people, but I'm not one of them. If you'd be so kind, I'd very much like you to come out and explain what you think you're *trying* to achieve here."

She waited.

Silence.

"No?" she added. "Well, that's disappointing but perhaps not entirely surprising. I must admit that I had hoped better of you."

Sighing, she glanced at the mirror again – and in that moment she saw not only her own reflection but also the reflection of a figure standing directly behind her. Despite the scratches and accumulated dirt on the mirror's surface, she was able to make out just enough of the figure's features to recognize her from the display in Emma Kemp's old bedroom.

"Help me!" the nurse gasped, clamping an icy hand over Rebecca's face and pulling her back. "Where are they?"

CHAPTER THIRTEEN

"NOTHING," JONATHAN MUTTERED, ONCE again passing the detector across the wall in an increasingly desperate attempt to find some evidence of an energy source. "Either it's well-hidden or..."

His voice trailed off as he stepped back and tried to come up with another option. Obviously actual ghosts were out of the question – that idea was simply too incredible for him to consider – so he assumed that some kind of trick had been used to generate the image of the children. He'd been more or less convinced that his detector would quickly find signs of a device hooked up to the window, yet now he realized that Ida Sinclair was clearly smarter than he'd anticipated.

And *much* smarter than she looked.

"How did you do it?" he whispered, thinking back to the sight of the children.

Stepping closer to the window again, he looked out again and once again saw the memorial in the distance. As he stared at the structure, however, he began to wonder whether something seemed a little wrong. He couldn't quite put his finger on the problem, but after a moment he took out his digital camera and held it up, quickly zooming in to take a better picture.

Once that was done, he brought the image up and zoomed in some more. The resolution was rather poor now, but it was sufficient to let him make out the memorial's approximate shape and -

Suddenly a scream rang out from somewhere nearby. Startled, he rushed to the door and looked out into the corridor. His heart was racing and deep down he already recognized the voice as belonging to his wife. The scream quickly faded away, only to be replaced by a series of frantic bumping sounds.

"Rebecca?" he called out, before hurrying along the corridor in a desperate bid to find her. "Rebecca, where are you?"

Reaching the top of a staircase, he hesitated as he heard more bumps and then he rushed down to the floor below. As soon as he got to the bottom he realized that the bumping sound was coming from a nearby room, and when he rushed to one of the doors he was immediately shocked to see Rebecca on the floor, curled into a ball in the corner and shivering.

"Rebecca, what's wrong?" he shouted, running over to her and dropping to his knees, then reaching out to put a hand on her shoulder. "Talk to me! What happened?"

"Get away from me!" she yelled, trying to push him back.

"Rebecca, it's me!" he hissed, grabbing her by the shoulders so that he could hold her in place. "What are you doing in here? Why did you scream?"

***

"I'm fine," she said a couple of minutes later, once she'd managed to regather her composure. "Jonathan, honestly, I'm completely okay. You don't need to keep fussing."

"You screamed," he pointed out.

"Only for a second or two."

"Rebecca -"

"I'm not immune to the shock value of... cheap theatrics," she added, interrupting him before taking his hand and allowing him to help her up from the floor. "She surprised me, that's all."

"Who did?"

She opened her mouth to reply, before

looking at the mirror. In that moment she once again saw the horrifying image of Emma Kemp standing just behind her, and she remembered the iciness of the dead woman's hand on her face.

No.

Not a dead woman.

Whoever had been in the room, she must have been alive.

"It was the nurse," she said, still struggling to force the last traces of fear from her voice. "Or rather, it was someone who had gone to great lengths to look like her. She put a hand on my face and she asked me where 'they' were, probably the children, and then..."

She paused as she tried to remember the precise sequence of events.

"I tried to pull away," she said cautiously, "but she was surprisingly strong. Finally she pushed me and knocked me over, and in the rush I'm afraid I lost sight of her. When I looked up again she was gone."

"You heard her running out of the room, I assume?"

"I'm not sure," she admitted. "No, I don't think so."

"Well, it's fairly obvious that she did," he pointed out. "There's nowhere else for her to have gone."

"I don't think it was Ida Sinclair, Jonathan,"

she replied. "If you're thinking that she dressed up as the dead nurse like some kind of... Scooby-Doo villain, then I'm really not sure it was anything so cheap. Besides, the resemblance was uncanny. The eyes were the same."

"Rebecca -"

"Don't worry," she added, "I'm not about to be convinced by some kind of parlor trick. I admit that the incident was quite well done, but I know it was merely an illusion."

Looking down, she spotted the scrap of paper on the floor. She picked it up and showed it to her husband.

"This slid out from under the door under there. Do you know what it might be?"

"There are some letters on it," he pointed out as footsteps approached the open doorway. "I feel as if I've seen something like this before, but I'm not sure where or -"

"Is everything alright?" Ida Sinclair asked, sounding a little breathless as she appeared in the doorway and looked through at them. "I heard a noise. It wasn't a scream, was it?"

"Where were you?" Jonathan asked.

"Me?" She seemed puzzled by the question. "I was in the kitchen, preparing tonight's meal. Why?"

"And you heard my wife crying out from all that way away?"

"I heard *something*," she told him, "but I couldn't really make out what it was." She looked around the room for a moment. "Did something happen in here?"

"Why?" Jonathan asked. "What do you think might have happened?"

"I really don't know," she replied cautiously, "but this is one of the parts of the house where people have reported... strange sensations from time to time."

"What's behind that door?" Rebecca said, gesturing toward the locked door on the far wall.

"In there?" Ida hesitated, before pulling a set of keys from her pocket and making her way over. "It's just the old reading room," she said, sorting through the keys and trying several in the lock. "It's empty now, like most of the rooms in this part of the house. Why, I haven't really thought about it in a good long time."

She tried a couple more keys before giving up and turning to them both.

"The correct key must be on another chain. I only carry the ones I use regularly, but I can fetch the key later and we can take a look."

"I'd like that," Rebecca replied, before holding the piece of paper up. "Have you ever seen anything like this before?"

"Well, it looks like..."

Ida paused again, and then she slowly

reached out and took the paper.

"It's part of an old ration card," she said. "I've seen plenty of them over the years during my research. Everyone in the country had these during the war." She turned the paper around. "Including children."

"Would they have brought the ration cards with them when they were evacuated here?" Rebecca asked.

"I assume so," Ida told her. "I'm no expert, though. Where exactly did you find it?"

"That doesn't matter right now," Rebecca replied, taking the scrap of paper back from her. "If you can find the keys to that door, though, I'd be very grateful."

"Did something happen to you in this room?" Ida asked.

"*Something*, yes," Rebecca admitted, "but we're still not quite sure what. I'd really rather take my time to figure out the details rather than rushing to conclusions."

"Did you see a ghost?" Ida continued, clearly keen to hear the details. "Was it her? Was it Emma Kemp, the nurse who died here? Did she -"

"Mrs. Sinclair, please," Rebecca said firmly, "my husband and I have a process and we must be allowed to follow that process. Initial reactions to events are rarely correct and often only add to the confusion. We're going to get to the bottom of this but in order to do so, we need to keep clear heads."

"I..."

Ida paused yet again, before taking a step back.

"Of course," she said after a few more seconds. "I wouldn't dream of interfering. You're the professionals and... and I should just keep out of your way and let you get on with things. I'm sorry if you feel I've been a little too pushy so far."

"That's fine," Rebecca said, still trying to study the woman's expressions and work out exactly whether she was being genuine.

"I've been preparing dinner," Ida continued, "and I hope that you're still planning to stay for another night. I understand if you want to leave, but Rose and I would very much like it if you'd stay with us."

"Of course," Jonathan told her. "We'd be delighted to stay. After all, we promised that we wouldn't leave until we've managed to get to the bottom of all this. We like to keep our promises."

"Although we're going to pop out for an hour or two," Rebecca said suddenly.

"We are?" Jonathan replied, clearly surprised by that news as he turned to her.

"Just briefly," Rebecca continued. "Sometimes we find that it helps to take a step or two back, just to get a better understanding of a situation. But we'll be back by, say, five this evening. Does that fit with your plans for dinner?"

"Absolutely," Ida said, although she was clearly still somewhat confused. "I hope you don't mind me asking, but... where exactly are you going?"

CHAPTER FOURTEEN

"THIS," JONATHAN SAID AS he watched the man at the bar raising a pint of ale to his lips, "might just be the best idea you've ever had in your entire life. But can't I have just one pint?"

"Not until we've got this figured out," Rebecca muttered, staring intently at the laptop's screen as she tried to come up with a moment of inspiration.

"But -"

"And you're driving."

"I know, but one pint won't be a problem."

"You need to be alert."

"One pint -"

"Jonathan, it's not happening."

"Sometimes we must savor the smallest things in life," he continued, watching as the man drank before taking a sip from his own glass of cola. "I've got to be honest, I wasn't expecting too much from this pub, but it has greatly exceeded my hopes."

Outside, the rain had stopped but a few drips were still falling occasionally from the top of the window.

"The temperature of that pint looks perfect," he added, almost salivating now as he watched the man still drinking the pint of ale, "and the color has this beautiful hue, as if the hops have been absolutely perfectly prepared, probably in a small batch and -"

"Got it!" Rebecca said suddenly, before turning the laptop around so that he could see the screen. "The six children who died at Marlstone Hall were evacuated between September and November 1939, as far as I can tell. Certainly they would have been in the first wave that began when the war broke out."

"Okay, so -"

"And they died almost immediately," she continued. "They all died before the end of the year."

"Yes, but -"

"Food rationing began in January 1940," she added, "so why would there be scraps of ration books floating around in the house, and why would they have anything to do with the children?"

"We don't know for certain that they do."

"It seems like the kind of mistake someone might make if they got sloppy," she suggested. "Plus Emma Kemp was dead by the start of rationing too."

"If -"

"And take a look at this," she continued, clicking through to another tab. "I didn't want to look this up while we were at the house, just in case Ida Sinclair has any way of monitoring what we're doing. But here's a photo of Emma Kemp taken in 1938."

She turned the laptop again so that he could see the sepia-tinted image of a smiling young woman.

"And?"

"It's not the same woman," she pointed out. "This certainly isn't the woman on the display board at Marlstone Hall. That image has clearly been faked."

"Why?"

"Why indeed?" she asked. "But it's the woman in the fake image who attacked me earlier today."

"So not the ghost of the real Emma Kemp, then."

"It didn't look like Ida Sinclair, but with enough make-up, I guess anything's possible."

"This still seems like quite a stretch," he

pointed out. "The risk of attacking you in broad daylight like that would have been extreme."

"I've done some more digging," she told him. "Although Emma was in charge of the children when they arrived, their care was ultimately in the hands of the local doctor, a guy named Crittenden. I did some research into Crittenden, and in 1948 he was struck off the medical register and sent to prison for falsifying medical records in order to obtain quantities of various drugs."

"For what reason?"

"It seems that he had a substance abuse problem of his own," she explained. "Most likely he was writing prescriptions and then handing out something entirely different, so that he could keep the real drugs for his own personal use. That might very well be why the treatment for the six children at Marlstone Hall didn't work. And then, to cover up his own crimes, Crittenden persuaded poor Emma Kemp that she was the one responsible. There seems to be little doubt from the available records that she committed suicide."

She waited for a reply, but for a few seconds Jonathan merely stared at the screen as if he was lost in thought.

"I can believe all of that," he said finally, "but there's one other matter that's been bugging me."

Pulling out his digital camera, he brought up

the grainy photo he'd taken of the memorial. Zooming in, he turned it around for his wife to see.

"The cross is there," he pointed out. "It wasn't when I went to take a closer look at the damn thing this morning."

"I'm pretty sure it was missing when I looked out the window earlier," she told him. "Do those bushes look the same, though?" She peered at the image for a moment longer before turning to her husband again. "I think we were looking in two different directions. There are two memorials."

***

"Jonathan Wheaton," Jonathan said later, once they'd returned to the house and had made their way round to find the second memorial, "Douglas Croft, Winifred Jones, Ernest Micklemore, Caroline Day and Meredith Pool. It's the same names as the first memorial. It's a memorial to the same tragedy."

"So why are there two?" she asked, looking past him and seeing the other memorial in the distance, with the cross on the top very much still broken. "One has been damaged and the other's brand new."

"But it's a copy of the first," he pointed out, stepping around the undamaged memorial and reaching out, giving it a gentle push. "Someone has gone to great lengths to recreate it, albeit for reasons unknown. But this one is newer."

"What if they're trying to conceal the damage to the original?" she suggested. "This one's slightly out of sight and it doesn't look like it's been properly set into the ground yet. It's only pure chance that we spotted it. What if it's waiting to be moved into place over there, to completely take the place of the original memorial?"

"Again, I just don't understand why," he told her, and now he sounded more than a little exasperated. "This is a lot of trouble to go to."

"The memorial's a key part of the story about this house," she continued. "It's in all the leaflets and on all the promotional material. If it's damaged, Ida couldn't simply pretend that it never existed. She'd either have to get it fixed or get a new one built. But this seems like the most expensive option, which seems odd given that she seems to be constantly short of money."

"I can't quite make my mind up about Ida Sinclair," Jonathan said as he continued to examine the newer memorial. "At first I had her down as an inveterate liar, just a scheming would-be toff trying to milk Marlstone Hall for all that it's worth. But now I'm starting to wonder whether she really knows what's going on at all."

"What are you suggesting?" she asked. "That someone else is responsible for the supposed haunting? The only other person here is Rose and she's only eight years old."

"The only other person we know of," he pointed out, looking at the house again. "Marlstone Hall is certainly very large and as Ida herself has pointed out, a lot of the place is closed off. What if somebody else is living in there and we just haven't noticed?"

"A hidden presence in the walls?" she suggested, raising an eyebrow.

"A hidden presence in one of the many abandoned rooms."

"There'd be signs," she replied. "That person would need to eat. To use the bathroom. To come and go."

"All of which could be concealed if somebody was desperate enough, and clever enough." He hesitated, still considering the possibility. "And if they had a little luck, they might be able to get away with it for quite some time. I doubt that they'd be very pleased about us showing up, however. And they wouldn't have been very pleased about old Martin Delaney coming here either. I know he supposedly destroyed all his notes before he died, but I can't help thinking that he's the key to all of this."

"In what way?"

"The guy was an absolute genius and a committed opponent of all things paranormal," he continued. "Then apparently he came here to

Marlstone Hall and he just... failed miserably. Sure, it's possible that his faculties deserted him as his illness progressed, but I'd like to know a little more."

"He spent his final days at his sister's home in Sheffield," she pointed out. "I know Sally Lupton from the university has been trying to get hold of some of his archives, but apparently the sister has been rather reluctant to cooperate. She even stopped replying to messages."

"Could you call Sally and get as much information as possible about that sister?" he replied. "I know there are rules against that sort of thing but, well, you and Sally are friends. I'm sure she'd be willing to help you out."

"What good do you think it'd do to contact her?" she asked. "If she's not responding to anyone at the university, what makes you think she'd pick up the phone and talk to a random stranger?"

"Nothing in the whole world," he admitted, "but fortunately that's not quite what I'm planning. There's something that has been bugging me about Martin Delaney's involvement in all this, and I think I know how to figure out exactly what's been going on. There's just one problem, Rebecca. Whoever's responsible – whether it's Ida Sinclair or someone else hiding in the house – we need to make sure that they don't suspect anything. And I'm afraid that means I need to ask you to do something."

"What's that?" she replied. "It's okay, you can tell me. If it's going to help us clear this mystery up, I'll do whatever you need me to do. Just name it."

CHAPTER FIFTEEN

"WELL," IDA SAID, SITTING at the head of the dining table that evening as she stared at the large pot of stew she'd prepared, "I suppose that's entirely understandable. After all, you and your husband are busy professionals and I suppose ghost-hunting doesn't really pay the bills, does it?"

"He asked me to convey his deepest apologies to you both," Rebecca replied, before glancing briefly at Rose and then turning to Ida again. "He didn't want to have to shoot of like this, but the call was very sudden. Apparently it's something to do with... funding deadlines."

"I imagine you have to deal with such things a lot," Ida said, before getting to her feet and starting to fill the first bowl with stew. "I suppose that simply means that there's a lot more food for the rest of us."

"That's fine by me," Rebecca said. "I'm starving."

"And you didn't need to go with him?" Ida asked.

"It's more his area of concern," she explained, worried that the woman's line of questioning was becoming a little too intense and persistent, "and besides, he wanted me to stay here and tie up some loose ends. Honestly, it's nothing to worry about."

"It doesn't sound to me like you're making much progress," Ida suggested.

"I admit that this house is a particular challenge," Rebecca told her. "Actually, I was wondering about Martin Delaney. I know he came here and tried to debunk the whole ghost story side of things, and I know he failed. That in itself is a big surprise given how thorough and methodical he was in most of his work. How long exactly did he stay?"

"Oh, a long weekend," Ida muttered, setting the bowl in front of Rose before starting to serve another. "Give or take. Much like you've been planning, actually. I must confess that Martin... Mr. Delaney was a rather strange fellow. Very intense and full of all these... nervous affectations. To be honest, I found his company quite unsettling and I was rather pleased that he chose to spend almost all his time in the other part of the house."

"Is that so?" Rebecca replied.

"Rose didn't much like him either, did you?" Ida continued, turning to her daughter. "Don't you remember that he was rather a... strange fellow?"

Rose stared at her mother for a moment before looking down, as if she was too timid to say very much at all.

"Well, he was," Ida added with a faint smile. "For one thing, he had a tendency to talk to himself. For another, he was very bad at explaining anything. He'd blurt out all this information to me and I wouldn't be able to understand half of it, and then he seemed to get rather irritated by me." She let out a heavy sigh. "I just tried to let him get on with things," she continued, "and Rose and I both stayed out of his way as much as possible."

"And then he... gave up?"

"He said he'd be returning," she explained, "but he didn't say when or anything like that. Eventually I called the university department up and asked if I could speak to him, which is when I learned that unfortunately he'd passed away. I know this is going to sound rather selfish of me, but I have to admit that my first thought was that all the fuss and bother had been for nothing. I'd been so hoping that he was going to publish a big paper confirming that Marlstone Hall is haunted, and that from there I could turn the place into a real success story."

"Did Mr. Delaney ever claim to have seen anything here?" Rebecca asked cautiously. "I find it hard to believe that he would, but..."

Her voice trailed off and she quickly realized that Ida seemed strangely reluctant to discuss the matter further.

"Not in so many words," Ida admitted finally, "but I could see it in his eyes. On the morning when he left, he was in such a hurry and he suddenly seemed so... skittish. If you ask me, he came here confidently expecting to prove that the whole thing was nonsense and then.... and then, yes, I believe that he saw something. I only wish that he'd stuck around for long enough to confirm as much. Then again, at least you're here now, so I suppose we have a second chance."

"I suppose we do," Rebecca said darkly, still trying to make sense of everything she'd just been told. "But if the great genius Martin Delaney couldn't figure it all out, I'm not sure that my husband and I have much of a shot."

***

"I was hoping to make the drive all in one go," Jonathan said over the phone as Rebecca stood in the bedroom, looking out at the pitch-black garden, "but I had to stop for petrol. I'll be on my way again soon. I should get to Martin Delaney's sister's place in the next hour."

"Sally warned me that the old woman's a bit of a demon," she murmured. "Don't be surprised if you just get the door slammed shut in your face."

"Don't you trust me to work my magic with charm and personality?"

"I'm sure you'll do the absolute best that you can," she told him with a faint smile.

"I'm really sorry again to have left you there like this. It's only for a few hours, though. I hope you understand."

"I'm not some delicate little thing who can't hold her own," she replied. "I've got to admit, though, I'm increasingly relieved that this is going to be our last haunted house investigation. I'd forgotten just how frustrating they can be. There's this big part of me that wants to get back to ordinary work again. How did we even get into this sideline in the first place?"

"We thought it'd be funny," he said with a deadpan tone, "and a fun way to relax. We thought we'd enjoy puncturing the egos of wannabe haunted house owners up and down the country."

"Yeah," she smiled, "and how's that working out for us?"

"I'm just glad you stopped me having that beer earlier," he said. "I'm tired enough as it is."

"If you're worried about falling asleep -"

"Relax, there's no way that's going to

happen," he told her. "I know that leaving you at the house alone was a big ask but -"

"Not this again," she sighed. "I'm fine, Jonathan, honestly. I'm going to spend the evening trying to talk to Rose a little more so that I can figure out what's happening. I might be wrong, but I feel like she clammed up at dinner as soon as her mother mentioned Martin Delaney. Something about her reaction wasn't quite right and I want to figure out exactly what's going on in her head. I get the feeling that she'll be a little easier to talk to than her mother."

Spotting a hint of movement in the darkness, she briefly wondered whether someone was walking across the lawn and heading toward the house. After a few seconds she realized that she must have been mistaken.

"I called mum earlier," she continued. "She said that Alicia's been really well-behaved and that there's no reason for us to worry. I told her that we'll try to get home tomorrow but that, if that's really not possible, it'll be Monday at the latest."

"Even if we haven't figured everything out at Marlstone Hall?"

She thought about that question for a moment.

"Yes," she said finally, "even if we haven't figured everything out at Marlstone Hall. There's comes a point at which we have to accept that we can't fix it all."

"And you can walk away? Even if little Rose -"

"You were right earlier," she said, cutting him off. "I need to separate my emotional response from the scientific side of what we're doing here. Sure, Rose Sinclair clearly isn't having the greatest childhood but that's true of almost everyone. She's not actually being mistreated, and she'll probably just grow up with all the usual problems that the rest of us have to deal with."

"That's not exactly what I -"

"So let's keep our heads in the game," she said firmly. "I don't like Marlstone Hall, Jonathan. The place is creepy as hell and I just want to get our job done and head home to Alicia. Then we can forget about this sort of thing once and for all. And remember, just because we might not prove that Ida's playing games, that doesn't mean we'll have failed. She's the one making the extraordinary claims. If she wants us to make a determination, she needs to come up with the goods at some point."

She watched the lawn for a moment longer, just to make sure that there was definitely nobody out there, and then she turned and headed back across the room.

"Call me later, once you've spoken to Martin Delaney's sister. Even if you don't get much out of her, there might be something useful. And I'll check in with Rose again. That girl must know a little more about the whole situation than she realizes. I just need to find a way to get through to her."

CHAPTER SIXTEEN

"HEY THERE, ROSE," REBECCA said as she stepped into the conservatory and saw the young girl sitting at the piano. "Was that you I just heard playing?"

"I don't *really* know how to play," Rose replied, looking down at the keys. "I was just being silly."

"No, it sounded good," Rebecca continued, making her way over to the piano. "There's no need to be shy. Is your mother around?"

Rose shook her head.

"Did she go out after dinner?"

"No, she just goes into the other side of the house usually."

"She does, huh?"

Stopping next to the piano, she looked down

at the girl. "Do you know why?"

"No," Rose replied. "She only started recently. She used to say that the cold side of the house was too horrible for anyone to ever want to go into, even the parts that are sometimes opened up for tourists. But lately she goes in there a lot and sometimes she's gone for hours and hours. I went to try to find her once but I couldn't work out where she was. Even in the cold side, there was no sign of her but I'm sure she was around somewhere. She had to be."

"And she leaves you all alone out here?"

"I don't mind, though. I don't mind being by myself. I prefer that to when I think there might be people around, and also I know that Mummy won't -"

Stopping suddenly, she seemed too scared to say more.

"You know that she won't do what?" Rebecca asked.

"Did you really not see them last night?" Rose continued. "When you found me in the room, I mean."

"You were in there by yourself."

She waited for a reply, but once again Rose seemed to be on the verge of saying something important.

"Weren't you?" Rebecca added. "Tell me something, Rose. When I came into the room, did you think you were talking to someone?"

"I don't know," she said, sounding increasingly shy.

"I think you *do* know," Rebecca told her. "It's okay, I won't make fun of you. I'd just really like to know."

"They're scared," she replied.

"Who are?"

"The children. They're like me. They're about my age, but they're scared. They've been in the house for a long time, since before I was even born, since before even Mummy was born. They're scared that something bad might happen if Mummy finds them."

"Is your mother looking for them?"

"She and the man were," she continued. "Mummy told the man all about the ghosts here, including the nurse too, and the man told her she was being silly."

"Are you talking about Martin Delaney?"

"They argued a lot but the man said he could prove it so he went to look around, a bit like you're doing. And then when he came out the next morning he looked really scared, and he talked to Mummy for a long time in the library, but... I wasn't supposed to listen."

"And *did* you listen?"

"I'm not normally naughty," Rose insisted.

"No-one said that you are," Rebecca replied,

and now she could see tears in the girl's eyes. Reaching out, she put a hand on her shoulder, hoping to offer at least a little reassurance. "But if you heard something interesting, I'd love to know what it is. What was she talking about with Mr. Delaney? Was she talking about a ghost?"

Rose hesitated, before shaking her head.

"Was she talking about her plans for the house?"

Again, Rose shook her head.

"Then what *was* she talking about?"

"You," Rose said cautiously, as if she knew that her mother would be furious with her for telling the truth. "She was talking to someone about you."

***

"Are you sure it was up here?" Rebecca asked as she led Rose up another set of stairs. "I thought this part of the house was more or less abandoned, just like the cold side."

"Mummy spent a lot of time up here just before you came," Rose said. "Some things came in a van and she had them brought up here. I think it's a new display about the history of the house."

"That wouldn't surprise me," Rebecca replied, reaching the top and looking both ways along the corridor. "It's quite clear that your mother sees the next tourist season as key to keeping the house going financially. If I was in her shoes, I'd be doing anything in my power to make the place interesting. Then again, I'm not sure that there's much more she *can* really do to turn it around."

"She was in that room," Rose whispered, clearly terrified as she pointed toward a door at the far end of the corridor.

"Are you going to come with me?" Rebecca said. "It's okay if you don't want to."

"I want to," Rose told her, although she seemed more than a little uncertain. "I think I do."

Making her way along the corridor, Rebecca realized that she had no idea what to expect. Reaching the door, she tried the handle and found that it opened easily enough. The next room was shrouded in darkness, but when she flicked a switch on the wall a set of lights burst to life, revealing several new displays that so far had been leaned against the walls as if they hadn't been properly put up yet.

"That's..."

As soon as she looked at the first of the panels, she realized that she could see a slightly grainy image of herself and Jonathan.

"That's us," she whispered.

Stepping closer, she saw a section of text next to the photo.

"Jonathan and Rebecca Pearson were ghost-hunters with a strong record of debunking claims of haunted houses," she read out loud from the panel. "In 2011 they came to Marlstone Hall hoping to prove that all the ghost stories about the house were false. What they discovered instead shook them to their core."

She turned to Rose.

"Your mother must have had these printed up weeks ago," she pointed out. "Months, even. And she's used photos taken from the university's website. She must be *very* confident that we're going to come out of this on her side."

Looking at the display again, she spotted another section of text.

"Over the course of a single weekend," she read, "the Pearsons became more and more concerned that they had finally discovered a genuine haunted house. As their old beliefs crumbled, they found themselves confronting a terrifying new reality – and the possibility that all the stories about ghostly goings-on at Marlstone Hall are true."

Moving the display panel aside, she found another, this time showing several grainy images of strange apparitions in the house's corridors. Under each image, a credit claimed that either she or Jonathan had taken the pictures.

"I've never seen these images before in my life," she murmured. "These displays boards are filled with outright lies."

Moving the panel up a little, she saw some more text.

"Gradually the Pearsons had no choice but to change their minds," she read. "Having always believed that they were right, they now had to acknowledge that Marlstone Hall's ghosts were indeed real. They even produced a series of images – reproduced here for the first time – in which they managed to capture evidence of the paranormal. Coupled with Martin Delaney's earlier work, the discoveries made by the Pearsons proved beyond a shadow of a doubt that something dark does indeed lurk in the shadows of this very house."

She turned to Rose again.

"This is all made up," she protested. "How does she ever expect to get away with misrepresenting our work in this way? Even if we *did* come to those conclusions, there's no way we'd simply stand back and let such an astonishing development become... just an exhibit in a small museum in the middle of nowhere. We'd have to work on a proper academic paper for years."

"Are you angry at Mummy?" Rose asked.

"I'm confused," she confessed. "My husband and I are respected researchers, we can't possibly allow our names to be used for something like this. After all twelve of our previous investigations we issued detailed reports explaining our findings and we certainly were planning to do the same thing here, but now I'm not sure that we should stay here for even another minute. I'm sorry, Rose, but your mother had absolutely no right to do any of this."

Rebecca turned to look at the displays again.

"This all has to stop right now," she said firmly. "We've allowed it to go too far. I don't know what your mother thinks she's playing at here, but it's almost as if she simply assumes that she can put words into our mouths. She's going to have to destroy these panels immediately and -"

"And what?" a familiar male voice asked suddenly, ringing out from the doorway. "Hello again, Rebecca. I hope you've been enjoying your time here at Marlstone Hall."

CHAPTER SEVENTEEN

AFTER SLAMMING THE CAR door shut, Jonathan turned and began to make his way along the poorly lit residential road until finally he spotted the door to number fourteen.

Stopping, he took a moment to try to work out exactly what he was going to say, and then finally – figuring that he'd traveled too far to let himself be delayed now – he knocked. Already he could hear the sound of a television running inside the property, and a few seconds later this was joined by the sound of someone opening the door.

Finally an elderly woman peered out at him with an expression that suggested she wasn't best pleased that she'd been disturbed.

"Hello," Jonathan said, trying to seem as friendly as possible, "I'm so sorry to disturb you at this late hour, but are you by any chance Mrs. Doreen Handley?"

"I am," she replied. "Do I know you?"

"No, but I know... I mean, I knew your brother Martin Delaney. Sort of. We were colleagues, although we didn't work together too closely. We certainly spoke many times, and I always took a great deal of interest in his work. Everyone at the faculty considered him to be something of a genius."

"Huh," she muttered dismissively. "You wouldn't think he was a genius if you'd had to put up with him the way I did."

She looked him up and down for a moment.

"What do you want, anyway?" she continued. "You're not here from the university to try to pressure me about his papers, are you? I won't be having any of that."

"Mum, are you okay?" a woman's voice called out from inside.

"They've sent someone to bloody have a go at me!" Doreen called out, clearly angry now. "I told 'em not to do it but they bloody well wouldn't take that for an answer, would they?" She raised a hand and jabbed a bony finger toward Jonathan's face. "You ought to be ashamed of yourself for disturbing me this late at night. You lot made your request to see his papers and I turned that request down. If you come here bothering me again, I'll ring the police and make sure you're arrested for harassment."

"I'm really not trying to harass anyone," he told her, fully aware that he'd already made a bad first impression. "Mrs. Handley, this is a rather urgent matter, I'm afraid. It's about an investigation that your brother carried out at -"

Before he could finish, she swung the door shut in his face, leaving him standing alone on the dark street.

"Marlstone Hall," he added with a sigh as he began to realize that his drive had been for nothing.

After knocking on the door again, he waited in the hope that Doreen might return. A few seconds later, however, he heard the television's volume going up and he understood that there was no way she was ever going to speak to him. Checking his watch, he turned and began to make his way back to the car as he tried to work out whether he might be able to make it back to Marlstone Hall by midnight. The whole trip had been a waste of time and -

"Hello?"

Turning, he saw a young woman hurrying out from an alley that ran down the side of the house.

"I'm sorry about Mum," the woman said, stopping next to him before glancing back at the front door as if she was scared that she might be spotted. "Is there somewhere we can go and talk?"

***

"I think it's really cool that you have this kind of side project where you hunt for ghosts," Katie Handley said as Jonathan set two coffees on the table and joined her in the booth. "Have you ever actually seen anything spooky?"

"I once saw a man in a padded cell try to eat a raw egg like it was an apple," he muttered, taking a seat opposite her. "That was pretty terrifying. But no, no ghosts."

"But you believe in them, right?"

"No, I absolutely don't."

"Why not?"

"Because they're clearly not real," he pointed out, feeling slightly disappointed that he was having to go through the same conversation again. How many times over the years had he been forced to defend his position? Why were so many people willing to believe in something for which there was absolutely no evidence whatsoever? "There's no credible support for the idea at all."

"But people have seen them."

"Nut-jobs and the deluded."

"Is that what you really think?" she asked, with the nervousness of someone who had clearly been about to launch into a ghost story of her own.

"I think people are complex," he continued,

trying to heed his wife's oft-repeated advice to be a little more diplomatic. "There are lots of reasons why someone might claim to have seen a ghost and some of those reasons are entirely well-intentioned."

He paused, and now he worried that he might sound a little too open to the idea.

"Most aren't," he added.

"I think there's something out there," she told him. "Something that we don't, or maybe even can't, understand. I think the reason there's no evidence for it is precisely the fact that it exists beyond our senses. Most of the time, anyway. Occasionally it drifts into our world and we get glimpses of it but... only glimpses. I just can't believe that when we die, that's the end."

He opened his mouth to reply to her, but at the last second he held back.

"You seemed very keen to talk to me," he reminded her, checking his watch again. "I don't mean to be rude, but I have quite a drive ahead of me."

"When Uncle Martin brought his boxes over for Mum to store," she continued, "he seemed different somehow. All the years when I was growing up, Uncle Martin was this... austere guy who couldn't tolerate anything that wasn't strictly logical. He didn't visit us very often, I think he considered us to be the common side of the family.

Whereas he went off to be this academic bigwig, Mum stayed behind and mostly did factory work, you know? So I think he looked down on us because he thought we weren't smart or something like that. Don't get me wrong, I always loved him to bits, but when he turned up with his boxes he was... panicking, somehow."

"Panicking?"

"On edge. Jittery. Like he'd seen a -"

She caught herself just in time.

"Mum noticed it too," she suggested. "Then he took her upstairs and I was told that I wasn't allowed to join them. I earwigged a bit, though, and I heard him explaining what he wanted her to do."

Reaching into her bag, she pulled out an A4 folder and set it on the table.

"Whenever Mum goes out, I go through those boxes." She slid the file toward him. "As soon as you showed up tonight, I just knew this was going to be about Marlstone Hall."

"And how did you know that?" he asked, struggling to put all the pieces together.

"Because that's what he was talking to her about," he continued. "Constantly. Over and over again, like a dog with a bone. He told her that he'd found something at Marlstone Hall, something that had changed his entire perspective. He told her that he needed time to figure it out but that eventually it was going to be a really big deal. And he told her that he wasn't sure when he'd be able to get back to see her again. It sounded like he was... saying goodbye, almost."

"He was very ill by that point, I believe?"

"Yeah, he'd begun to get sick. It was really sad." She paused again. "I was really struck by how much he was begging Mum to help him. He'd *never* talked to her like that before. And after he left, she was... different, somehow. She just didn't want to talk about him, not at all, and she got angry any time I brought him up. If she knew that I'd been sneaking into that room and looking through his files, I honestly think she'd never forgive me."

"Why does she feel so strongly about that?"

"I'm really not sure," she admitted, "but he's pulled her into something big, and I'm not sure she's entirely comfortable with it. He told her that she's going to be taken care of, though. I didn't hear everything they were talking about, but he definitely told her that financially she's going to be sorted out for good. And I've spotted her looking at some pretty expensive houses online, like she's starting to think about moving."

"What's in this file?" he asked.

"It's his notes about Marlstone Hall," she explained. "And a memory stick, too. You should watch it. I need to get home soon, but don't worry, the notes are a copy I made. The original's still in his boxes. I wouldn't risk taking the original."

"In case your mother found out?"

"Or Uncle Martin," she added, and now there was genuine fear in her voice. "That's the part of all this that I never liked, and I think it's the part that Mum hates too. Uncle Martin's still alive. I know he got Mum to tell people he'd died, but none of that's true. He's still alive and whatever he's up to, it's all about Marlstone Hall."

CHAPTER EIGHTEEN

"IT'S BEEN A WHILE, hasn't it?" Martin Delaney said, stepping into the room and glancing at the displays featuring the Pearsons. "When did we last speak, Rebecca? Was it at Ron Findley's Christmas drinks thing last year?"

"What are you doing here?" Rebecca asked, taking a step back. "Martin, you... you died."

"A necessary little deception on my part," he muttered, stopping to look at one of the display panels as Ida followed him into the room. "I realized quite early on that I was going to have to go to extreme lengths in order to complete my work here at Marlstone Hall."

"There was a funeral," she stammered.

"My sister was very useful when it came to concocting the lie," he admitted, turning to her with a faint smile. "She really didn't like the idea, but I told her that it was really only one *little* lie, and that it'd all be worth it in the end. Poor Doreen really isn't very worldly, I'm afraid I was the one who got the brains in our family but... well, that's not really fair. Doreen's a good woman and she doesn't like lying, but I managed to talk her round."

"You faked your death," Rebecca replied cautiously, "and... you've been hiding here ever since?"

"I think you almost spotted me earlier, didn't you?" he asked. "When I was heading back inside you were at one of the windows and I thought for a moment..."

He watched her carefully, as if he was trying to work out just how much she knew.

"Or perhaps not," he added with a chuckle, before turning to Ida. "Darling, why don't you put little Rose to bed? She shouldn't be up this late, should she?"

"Of course not," Ida replied, hurrying over to Rose and grabbing her hand before starting to lead her from the room. "Come on, Rose. It's way past your bedtime."

Glancing over her shoulder as she left the room, Rose looked one last time at Rebecca before disappearing from view.

"Ida's a good woman," Martin explained once he was alone with Rebecca. "She's been through so much and the pressure of trying to maintain this house almost broke her. By the time I arrived to investigate her claims, it was clear that she was on the verge of some kind of emotional breakdown. She might even have been in the early stages of one. The point is, I immediately took a liking to her and we've certainly grown... closer during my time here."

"Martin, what's going on here?" she asked. "Everyone thinks you're dead!"

"Perhaps I am," he replied. "Perhaps the man you see before you now is a mere ghost."

He hesitated, before stepping toward her and putting a hand on the side of her arm.

"Do I feel like a ghost?" he added. "No? Good, because I'm not. I'm certainly sick, that much is true, but I exaggerated the progression of the condition. I have a little longer left than I wanted anyone to know. The truth is, once I arrived at Marlstone Hall, everything changed. It was as if, as they say, the scales fell from my eyes. For the first time, I could see properly and I understood that I was on the verge of a great discovery."

"Martin -"

"Let me prove it to you," he continued eagerly, and now his eyes were filled with a sense of great excitement. "There are ghosts here, Rebecca. *Real* ghosts. We were all wrong about it before. Ghosts exist and here at Marlstone Hall we're going to prove that fact to the world!"

***

Although she desperately wanted to call Jonathan and tell him to get back quickly, Rebecca instead allowed Martin to lead her deeper into the colder side of the house. She still hadn't entirely wrapped her head around the reality of the situation – around the fact that Martin Delaney had faked his own death – and she couldn't help thinking back to the shock surrounding his passing.

"Such a pity," one of her colleagues had said, seemingly close to tears, when the news had first spread across the campus. "He had such a great mind."

"The departments will never be the same again," another colleague had opined despondently. "He just had such an exquisite intellect. Someone should organize a fundraiser. We need to name a building after him."

"You're being very quiet," Martin said now, sounding slightly pleased with himself as he pushed open another door and led her into a room – the same room with the mirror in which she'd seen the strange woman. "You must be deep in thought."

Stopping, he turned to her with a broad smile.

"Did you happen," he continued, "to attend

the lecture I gave at the Robert Rosenberry memorial conference last... November? I think it was November, anyway. Or was it October? I'm really not sure. I've been giving so many lectures and presentations of late."

Slowly, she shook her head.

"Pity," he muttered, "because that would have brought you up to speed. I devoted a large part of that lecture to the need for novel experimental parameters. Not every investigation has to start and finish in some kind of... laboratory or examination room. Sometimes we have to venture beyond our comfort zones."

"By pretending to be dead?"

"In this case, yes," he told her. "Absolutely nothing should be beyond consideration. I'm fully aware of my reputation, Rebecca. Over the years I've come to be regarded as something of a... I mean, I only use this word because others have proposed it, but... I have been referred to many times as a genius. I happen to not believe that I *am* a genius, but that's not really relevant. The point is, my reputation precedes me and I decided to put that to good use."

"By letting people think that you've made some great discovery?"

"No, by letting them think that I've failed," he countered. "Admit it, the news spread like wildfire. People just loved to gossip about the fact that – in his final moments – the great Martin Delaney had finally been broken by a case. That I'd uncovered a supposedly haunted house that I couldn't debunk. There must have been a certain segment of the academic staff that enjoyed my downfall. Schadenfreude can be a powerful thing and people are much more gullible when they're asked to believe a lie that they enjoy."

"We heard that before you died, you failed to crack Marlstone Hall," she told him.

"That's exactly what I *wanted* you to hear," he replied. "And I happened to have learned that you and your husband were dabbling in precisely the same field. So what, I wondered, would happen if the poacher became the gamekeeper? What if, instead of being the one bumbling about in yet another cold old English house, I could be the one overseeing the whole thing?"

"So you... manipulated us so that we'd come here?"

"I certainly hoped that you would."

"And you've been watching us ever since?"

"I understand why you might be unhappy," he continued, "but think of it another way. It's really as if I offered to recruit you as my assistants. I've been *supervising* you."

"We don't want to be anyone's assistants," she told him.

"Which is precisely why I had to conduct

my experiment in this manner," he insisted. "To be honest, I hoped to keep my presence hidden for a little while longer, but I probably should have known that I couldn't pull the wool over your eyes forever. Even though we haven't had the chance to do much work together, Mrs. Pearson, I know of your work. And your husband's work too. I admire you both very much."

"Thanks," she said cautiously, "but I'm still not seeing the bigger picture here."

"Where did your husband go today?" he asked. "I confess that I didn't quite catch that part."

"Just... out for a few hours," she replied, figuring that she didn't necessarily need to tell him everything. Not just yet, at least.

"Will he be back soon?"

"He should be."

"He's gone to visit my sister, has he not?"

"I really couldn't say," she replied, even though she suspected that he knew the truth only too well.

"Then he's in for quite a shock," Martin continued. "The truth is, I became rather lost in my research here at Marlstone Hall. I started to doubt my own senses. Even video and audio evidence began to seem untrustworthy to me. I realized eventually that I needed to step aside and observe another investigation, which is why I brought you here. And so far, just as I expected, the process has been most worthwhile. Most worthwhile indeed."

"This is one of the least ethical things I've ever heard of," she told him.

"Who cares about any of that?" he asked. "Mrs. Pearson, I'm about to show you the greatest ever experiment in the field of paranormal research. And when you see what I've been up to here, you'll realize that my decision to involve you and Jonathan is a great honor."

Slipping a key from his pocket, he headed over to the door on the far side of the room. He took a moment to unlock the door, and then he turned to her.

"Well?" he continued, as he turned the handle and the door began to click open. "Are you ready to meet them?"

"Them?" she replied, feeling as if her mind was racing now. "Who are you talking about?"

"Who do you think?" he asked, pushing the door all the way open to reveal six withered corpses on tables in the next room. "The children, of course."

CHAPTER NINETEEN

"MUMMY, WHO'S THAT MAN? Is it..."

Stopping as she reached the doorway, Ida hesitated for a few seconds before slowly turning to her daughter. Rose was sitting up in bed, having evidently failed to obey her instructions to simply go to sleep.

"Mr. Delaney is... a friend, Rose," she said cautiously. "You met him before. Don't you remember?"

"Yes, but he looks scruffier now. And I thought he went away."

"He did go away, but then he... he came back."

"When?"

"I don't have time to go into all of this right now," Ida complained. "Sweetheart, I'm getting a headache and I just need you to go to sleep."

"Is he upset with Mrs. Pearson?"

"Why would you ask that?"

"Has he been hiding here?"

"Rose -"

"*Has* he, Mummy?" she continued. "Why would he have been hiding here? Sometimes I heard someone in the cold part of the house, but I didn't know it was him."

"Martin's here to help us," Ida said firmly. "It's too complicated for you to understand, you're just a little girl, but Martin is a very kind and generous soul. He's a real gentleman, in fact. As he and I got to know each other last time, we both realized that we might be able to help one another. I have this wonderful house that just needs a little help so that it can be profitable, and he has his life's work. Together we can be much more successful than either of us could ever have managed alone."

"Do you like him?"

"Of course I like him," she replied, unable to hide a sense of irritation. "What kind of question is that, Rose?"

"I never..."

For a moment, Rose seemed reluctant to speak, yet something seemed to be spurring her on.

"I never knew Daddy," she said finally. "I've never even seen a photo of him, or of anything from when I was little. Is Mr. Delaney anything like

Daddy?"

"No," Ida said, shaking her head gently, "Martin is *nothing* like your father, and this conversation has gone on for far too long now. It's way past your bedtime, young lady, and I'm not going to stand here answering an endless stream of questions. I want you to put your head down and go to sleep, and in the morning I want you to just let the adults get on with things, okay?"

"Okay," Rose said softly, although she was clearly unhappy about the arrangement.

"I've got enough on my plate without having to listen to all your nonsense," Ida muttered, bumping the door shut and then walking away from the room, still talking to herself under her breath.

Still sitting on the bed, Rose knew that she should do as she'd been told, yet at the same time she wasn't remotely tired. Hearing an owl hooting outside, she turned and looked at the window, and now she felt more than ever that she was missing out on everything that was happening. As much as she wanted to obey her mother, she couldn't help thinking about the six children in the other side of the house, and part of her worried that something terrible was going to happen to them if they were ever found.

Finally, despite a sense of dread in her chest, she began to slowly climb out of bed.

***

"I heard something up ahead," Martin said, his voice coming over loud and clear from the laptop's speakers as the video continued to play. "I can't be sure, but..."

Sitting in his car, with the laptop balanced on the passenger seat, Jonathan continued to watch the screen. He'd been flicking through the papers in the folder Katie had handed him, but in truth he'd found Martin Delaney's spider-like handwriting rather difficult to decipher. Instead he'd finally slipped the memory stick out from the envelope and had plugged it into his laptop, and he'd quickly discovered that it contained a set of videos that Martin had made during his visit to Marlstone Hall.

So far, these videos were unlike anything Jonathan had seen before. Despite Martin's reputation for scientific rigor, the man seemed genuinely terrified as he made his way along the dark corridors of the old house.

"It was somewhere round here," the man on the screen said now, pushing open another door and shining a flashlight into one of the many nondescript rooms. "I might be wrong," he continued, as his voice became tighter and tighter with tension, "but I think it came from in here."

For the next couple of minutes, the video was mostly silent – save, that is, for the sound of

Martin's footsteps as he slowly made his way around the room. Although the space was quite clearly empty, Jonathan realized that Martin seemed utterly determined to check every corner over and over again, as if he was completely convinced that eventually he was going to find something of note.

"This doesn't seem like you," Jonathan whispered. "The Martin Delaney I met all those times wouldn't act like this, he'd be way too skeptical."

"I've noticed a significant decrease in the temperature," Martin said suddenly, turning the camera around so that it was pointing directly into his own face. "Just in the past couple of minutes, the temperature in this room must have dropped ten degrees at least."

"I'm not surprised, in that place," Jonathan said under his breath. "The insulation must be -"

"There!" Martin gasped, swinging the camera around and aiming the flashlight at the doorway, just as a set of footsteps could be heard hurrying away. "There's definitely someone here!"

He ran to the doorway and looked out into the corridor, but there was no sign of movement. He waited, constantly turning the camera around as if he still expected to catch something worthwhile, before finally he once again peered directly into the lens.

"I'm going to admit something right now,"

he said, and now his voice was shaking a little. "I'm not entirely sure that I can explain whatever's going on here. I know that it's not Mrs. Sinclair, and that her young daughter is safely in the other side of the house. *Someone* is definitely in here with me, and I'm starting to think that they're playing with my senses. After all, they could easily avoid me if they wanted to but -"

Before he could finish, a loud and strangely heavy gurgling sound filled the air in the video, lasting for several seconds before ending as abruptly as it had begun.

"What the hell was that?" Martin whispered, turning and aiming the camera at a nearby open door. "It sounded like -"

In that moment the sound returned, seemingly a little louder and more insistent than before; it lasted for several more seconds, and this time it ended much more slowly. The gurgle began to fade away until it became nothing more than a series of spluttering gasps.

"It's in there," Martin said, struggling to hold the camera still now as he continued to aim it at the doorway. "I've never been certain of anything in my life."

He began to step toward the door, although he slowed his pace a little as he approached – as if fear had begun to creep its way into his thoughts.

"Hello?" he called out. "Is anyone there?

I'm not in the mood for playing games. My name is Doctor Martin Delaney and, among other things, I'm a senior research in the fields of psychiatry and parapsychology. If you think you can fool me, you're very quickly going to learn that you've met your match. So you might as well save us both a lot of trouble and come out of the woodwork."

As he swung the camera around, his erratic breaths could be heard. Although he was tempted to end this particular video and check the others before setting off on the drive back to Marlstone Hall, Jonathan told himself that he could spare just a few more minutes.

And then, slowly, the gurgling sound returned to the speakers. This time, however, it sounded more like a low rattle, and a moment later the camera stopped moving almost entirely.

"I know you're there," Martin said as a sense of genuine dread crept into his voice. "I'm not afraid of you. Whatever you are, you have to understand that I'm not afraid of anything at all. So whatever you think you're going to do here, I need you to realize that you're going to fail."

With that, he hesitated for a few seconds before slowly starting to turn around while keeping the flashlight's beam raised. A few seconds later the camera picked out what appeared to be a young boy standing directly behind him, letting out the gurgles from the back of his throat as the light bleached his pale features in its glow.

Jonathan leaned forward.

"What the -"

Before he could finish, the video came to a sudden halt.

Sitting alone in the car, he could only stare at the screen as he tried to make sense of what he'd just seen. After watching a set of cliched empty rooms as the video had proceeded, at the very end he'd suddenly been presented with the sight of a boy who'd looked like something straight out of a horror movie. The image would have been laughable had it not been for the fact that it had been so direct. There had been no attempt to hide the figure away or to make it harder to distinguish. Instead it had been right there, framed almost perfectly, until the video had ended.

Grabbing his phone, he brought up Rebecca's name and tried to get a call through, only to be immediately sent to voicemail once more. He'd attempted to call his wife several times since meeting Katie, and he could only assume that signal coverage at Marlstone Hall – especially at night – wasn't too great.

"Rebecca, I'm on my way back right now," he said, trying to stay calm even as he realized that Delaney might well be at the house. "When you get this, call me back immediately. And Rebecca... Martin Delaney's still alive. You have to be careful."

CHAPTER TWENTY

"IT'S ALRIGHT, REBECCA," MARTIN said, making his way between the tables and looking down at the withered, partially skeletal remains. "There's absolutely no risk of infection, not after all this time. You can't catch typhus from a corpse that has been dead for almost a century."

"Are these..."

Stopping just inside the doorway, Rebecca saw the body of a young girl dressed in faintly old-fashioned clothing. Her first assessment had been that the bodies had been mummified somehow, but now she realized that for the most part they'd simply lost the majority of their flesh, with just a few patches clinging to the exposed bones. And as she looked around at the other dead children, she felt a shiver run through her bones.

"Let me guess," Martin said wearily, "you're about to tell me that I can't do this, or that I shouldn't do it, or that I'm some kind of monster."

With tears in her eyes, she turned to him.

"Say what you want," he continued. "See if I care. All that concerns me is the result of the experiment, which I happen to believe is going to be extremely interesting."

"You dug them up?" she stammered, scarcely able to believe what she was seeing. "You took them out of their graves?"

"Isn't that obvious by now?" he asked. "Of course I did. Some sentimental fool had seen fit to bury them beneath the memorial, which was certainly convenient."

Stepping over to one of the tables, she saw the skeletal remains of a young boy. She instinctively reached out to touch his shoulder, before holding back at the last second. His mouth had been left slightly open while his empty eye sockets looked over toward the far wall.

"They're here," Martin said firmly.

Rebecca turned to him.

"I don't just mean physically, as in the bodies," he continued. "I mean they're *here* in a very different sense as well. This might come as a bit of a shock to you, Rebecca, but I myself have seen several of them. I've seen them as they were in life, inhabiting rooms in this very house. I've seen their ghosts."

Slowly, she began to shake her head.

"Don't be so quick to judge me," he told her. "That's very unscientific, is it not? My witness testimony most certainly counts as primary evidence."

"These are *children*," she pointed out, struggling to contain a sense of fury. "They were buried and now you've disturbed them! You've ripped them out of their graves!"

"So?" he asked, raising an amused, skeptical eyebrow. "You profess to not believe in any kind of spiritual aspect to the human mind. You seem to abhor the very idea of the soul, and you're certainly in no way religious. So why do you care if the children have been disinterred? Based on your love of scientific rigor, as you put it, shouldn't you see these corpses as being nothing more than a collection of bones?"

"I believe in souls!" she snapped back at him.

"Really?" He tilted his head to one side. "Are you sure about that? You can't measure a soul, Rebecca. You can't weigh it or determine its value. You can't even look at it. You and your husband are renowned as adherents of the scientific principle. How can you possibly claim, then, to see these corpses as anything more than mere relics of lives long ended?"

"They're children!"

"So *you're* being sentimental too," he added with a faint, sneering smile. "That's exactly what I thought."

"This is wrong," she replied, taking a step back before turning and storming out of the room. "I'm going to call the police! Whatever you think you're doing here, it ends tonight!"

***

"Damn it, come on!" Rebecca snapped as she hurried out from the front of Marlstone Hall and stopped to tap her phone again. "You were fine earlier!"

She waited for the phone to connect, yet still she found that she had no network. Holding the phone up, she waited in case some bars finally appeared, and then she let out a sigh as she realized that she wasn't going to be able to simply call 999 and get help. And with Jonathan having taken the car, she began to wonder whether she was going to have to walk all the way to the nearest village.

"We're not bad people."

Turning, she saw a figure stepping out of the shadows.

"Truly we're not," Ida Sinclair continued, with tears in her eyes. "I get it, you're shocked but... please try to see this from my point of view."

"There are six dead children on tables in your house!" Rebecca snapped angrily.

"They've been dead for decades," she replied. "Seventy-two years, I believe, if I've got my sums right."

"When's the cut-off point? After how long does it become acceptable?"

"They're so old," Ida insisted. "They're barely even recognizable."

"That doesn't change anything," Rebecca told her. "Did you know that it's illegal to disturb a grave in this country?"

"Even if the grave isn't in a churchyard?"

"You can't do this!" Rebecca hissed. "How can you condone it all? You're a mother!"

"Well, I..."

Ida's voice trailed off for a few seconds, and then she took a couple more steps forward.

"I had a replica of the memorial made," she insisted. "That was the one thing I insisted on. Martin damaged the original memorial when he removed the body but I told him that we had to get an exact copy put back in its place. It's here now and ready to be moved into position soon, just as soon as the old one is gone. You have to understand that I never wanted to disrespect anyone, so I paid for the new memorial myself."

"Their bodies are laid out in a room!" Rebecca pointed out.

"It's just temporary," Ida replied, and now a solitary tear was running down one cheek. "Martin's got it all worked out. We're going to draw the children from the shadows so that he can study them properly, and then everyone will know that Marlstone Hall is the first true, provable haunted house in the whole world. And once that's done, Martin has promised me that the children will be reburied beneath the new memorial. Everything will go back to how it was before, but with one crucial difference. Marlstone Hall will have been saved forever."

"As a tourist attraction?"

"As the place where ghosts were first discovered. Provably real ghosts, at least. Martin has worked out how to tease them from the shadows."

Rebecca began to shake her head.

"No, it's true!" Ida continued. "I've seen them too! It's taken a lot of work, but he's finally managed to figure out how to lure them into the light. He managed to catch them on film before, very briefly, but they always cause the image to glitch. He's figured out a way to avoid that now. He's such a genius and I have total faith in him. He even came up with a whole narrative to make people more interested."

"A narrative?" Rebecca replied. "What are you talking about?"

"He sees the bigger picture," she explained, and now her eyes seemed almost to be glowing with excitement. "When I told him all my ideas for Marlstone Hall, he took them and ran with them and made them ten thousand times better. He showed me that this house has so much more potential than I ever realized. And most of all, he showed me that we have a future here. Rose and I can build something really important if we just let him guide us. And then... and then he's going to stay here with us and help to make it so much better. As husband and wife, we can achieve anything we want!"

"Husband and wife?" Rebecca said cautiously.

"We've... grown closer since he first came to the house," she replied, and now she seemed embarrassed, almost blushing. "Honestly, I never thought I'd get another chance at love. I thought I was destined to die alone, and I certainly didn't think that a man as brilliant as Martin Delaney would ever want me. But he says... he says he sees something in me. Something special. Something that no-one – not even my ex-husband – has ever seen before. My life is going to start all over again and I'm finally going to be happy."

"We'll see about that," Rebecca said, checking her phone again and seeing that she'd finally managed to get some signal. Turning, she held the phone up and tapped to make a call. "I'm sorry, but I can't just stand by and watch as -"

Before she could finish, Ida smashed a metal poker against the side of her head, knocking her out cold and sending her body crumpling down to the ground. The phone slid across the patio, and Ida grabbed it and canceled the call before it had a chance to connect.

"I'm sorry about that," she said as she looked down at Rebecca's unconscious form next to her feet, "but Martin warned me that I might have to be a little forceful with you. And it's all going to be worth it in the end. Even though things are slightly rushed now, it's pretty much going exactly the way he promised it would."

CHAPTER TWENTY-ONE

Six months earlier...

"SHE'S ASLEEP," IDA SAID, stopping in the doorway and looking through into the library, where Martin was studying some more papers. "I'm still not sure that this is a good environment for her, though. I'm sure she picks up a lot more than I've been telling her."

"Hmm?" he replied, not even glancing up. "What are you talking about?"

"Rose," she continued, heading over to him. "I've tried to shield her from things as much as possible but she's such an intelligent girl. Are you sure it wouldn't be better if I... sent her away somewhere for a few weeks?"

"Weeks?"

Finally he looked up at her.

"What good would weeks do?" he asked.

"Well, just until this is over."

"It won't be over in weeks," he told her. "Do you seriously not understand how much work we've got ahead of us? We can't establish an entire ghost story here at Marlstone Hall in a matter of weeks. This is going to take months, perhaps even a year or two."

"Can't we hurry it up a little?"

"Absolutely not," he replied, looking at the papers again. "I'm starting to sketch out a timeline. I know just the people to lure here, they think they're ghost-hunters but in truth they're just amateur hobbyists. But they're essential, because we need someone to have real skin in the game. I've come up with a plan, although I have to admit that it's going to require a great deal more hard work than I initially believed. I'm going to have to..."

His voice trailed off as he turned one of the papers over.

"Are you sure this isn't a mistake?" she asked. "Martin, you know I'd do anything to save Marlstone Hall, but I'm worried that this might be a step too far. I don't want to lie to people or -"

"People love being lied to," he replied quickly, cutting her off. "They lap these things up. Don't worry about that."

"But all this deception -"

"I told you, leave it to me," he said firmly. "All you have to do is play the hostess when I bring certain people here, and I'll take care of the rest. And I know from experience that you can be an *excellent* hostess."

Glancing up at her, he saw that she was unconvinced. After a moment he reached out and placed a hand on her waist.

"When I came here," he continued, "I was so sure that the whole set-up was just another trick. No other possibility even entered my mind. It took a while for me to come around to the idea that there might be real ghosts at Marlstone Hall, but now that I'm a believer, I'm in this all the way. Fortunately I'm willing to do the things that seemed like too much for you. You've achieved so much, Ida, and I'm going to push it over the finish line for you. For us."

Getting to his feet, he headed to a small table and fetched two glasses of whiskey. Carrying them back over, he kissed Ida's cheek before handing her one of the glasses and then kissing her on the cheek.

"The day I met you," he whispered softly, "has turned out to be the greatest day of my life, both personally and professionally. I'm so grateful for everything you've helped me with, Ida. You've changed my entire view of the world." He paused, looking deep into her eyes, before taking a sip of whiskey from his glass. "Drink," he continued. "Heaven knows, you deserve it after a day like today."

She took a long sip, finally finishing the whole glass in one go.

"That's better," he said with a smile. "You'll be feeling tired soon. Why don't you go to bed and I'll be up to join you soon? I just need to work out a few more of these ideas while they're still fresh in my mind." He kissed her once more on the cheek. "And when this is all over," he added, "we'll have more time for each other. I promise."

***

Standing at the bedroom door a short while later, Martin looked through into the darkened room. He could just about make out Ida's slumbering form on the bed, and after a few seconds he stepped back and gently bumped the door shut.

"That stuff should keep you knocked out until morning," he said under his breath. "It usually does."

Heading along the corridor, he was already working on the next part of his idea. By the time he reached the door to Rose's room, he felt sure that he had everything under control. After pushing the door open and seeing that the girl was asleep, he glanced over his shoulder one more time – just to check that Ida wasn't about to disturb him – before slipping into the room and making his way to the bed.

"Rose," he said softly, dropping to his knees and gently touching her shoulder. "Rose, it's me. Don't be scared."

Slowly opening her eyes, Rose stared back at him.

"Hey there, Rose," he continued with a smile. "I'm so terribly sorry to have woken you up but, well, I need your help with something. Your mother's sleeping. Do you think you might be able to get up and come through to the other side of the house with me?"

Sitting up, Rose continued to stare at him as if she didn't quite understand.

"Come on," he said, grabbing her by the hand and forcing her to stand up, then leading her out of the dark bedroom and into the well-lit corridor. "That's right. I'm so sorry to get you up in the middle of the night like this but, well, I need to film something. You understand, don't you?"

"Where's Mummy?" Rose asked, sounding exhausted.

"I told you, your mother's asleep."

"She told me that I'm not supposed to get up in the middle of the night."

"And quite right too," he continued, leading her to a door and pushing it open, then taking her into the cold side of the house. "You mustn't *ever* get up in the night alone. You must only do it when you have an adult with you."

"It's cold in here," she said cautiously.

"You trust me, Rose, don't you?" he added, speeding up a little as he led her toward the corridor's far end and then around the corner. "I know you do. I only want to make things perfect for you and your mother, and that means doing a few things that... well, I suppose they might seem a little strange to you, but that's because you're so young. There just isn't time for me to explain it all, which means I'm simply going to tell you what to do and you're going to do it. Doesn't that sound nice and fair?"

"I want to talk to Mummy."

"No, you really don't."

After leading her along several more corridors, he finally took her into one particular room, where he'd already set out several items on a table. Letting go of her hand, he grabbed a flashlight and switched it on, and then he carried a wig back across the room and began to arrange it on top of Rose's head.

"You'll have to give me a few minutes," he muttered, "because even though you'll only be in the shot very briefly, it's important that no-one spots you. Fortunately I've done my research and I know what angles to use. Once I'm done, even your own mother would struggle to recognize you."

"I don't know what you mean."

"Hold this."

He forced the flashlight into her hands and then muttered to himself as he continued to adjust the wig, and then he headed back to the table.

"You're going to be dressing up as a boy for a few minutes," he explained. "I've already filmed the rest of this little encounter, and I did it in a way that's going to make it easy for me to drop in the final shot. The miracle of hidden edits, eh? All you have to do is look up at me. That's easy enough, isn't it?"

Rose opened her mouth to answer, but at the last second she heard a whispering sound coming from nearby. Turning, she looked at the open doorway; at first she saw no sign of anyone, but after a few more seconds she realized that she could just about make out something shifting behind the door, seemingly peering through at her from a spot behind the hinges. Squinting, she tried to make the figure out and -

"Here," Martin said suddenly, grabbing her shoulder and forcing her to turn to him. "Put this on. It's just an old sack, really, but the belt should make it look like something a poor child would have worn during the war."

She looked over at the doorway again, only for Martin to put a hand on her jaw and force her around again.

"Keep your head in the game, Rose," he said firmly. "You can be back in bed in just a few minutes from now, just so long as you help me out here. I simply need you to stare up gormlessly at me for a few minutes. Can you do that?" He waited for an answer, before patting her on the shoulder. "That's it," he continued, pulling his phone out and getting ready to start filming. "Get into the little costume I made for you and then we can hopefully shoot the whole thing in just one take."

Rose looked at the doorway again, but this time she saw no sign of anyone. After a few seconds, supposing that Martin knew best and that she really shouldn't ask too many questions, she began to search for some way to slip the sack over her head.

"And this has to stay between the two of us, okay?" Martin continued. "Your mother's very stressed at the moment so she doesn't need to know. Let's just keep it as our little secret."

CHAPTER TWENTY-TWO

Six months later...

AFTER SLAMMING THE CAR door shut, Jonathan Pearson turned and began to make his way up toward the main door of Marlstone Hall. His mind was racing and he was still trying to make sense of everything he'd discovered, but as he stepped into the main hall he knew that there was only one person who could answer all his questions.

"Martin?" he called out, stopping at the foot of the main staircase. "Martin Delaney, I know you're here. What the hell's going on?"

He waited, but all he heard in response was silence.

"Rebecca?" he continued, pulling out his phone but quickly finding that now he too had no signal. "Damn it Rebecca, what -"

"You're back."

Startled, he turned to see Ida watching him from the shadows.

"You poor thing," she said, stepping closer. "You must have had such a long drive. It's gone midnight, why don't you let me -"

"Where's Martin Delaney?" he snapped. "And where's my wife?"

"Everything's absolutely alright," she said coolly, holding her hands up as if she felt that this would in some way calm him down. "You really mustn't get yourself so worked up, Mr. Pearson. I'm sorry if certain omissions had to be made in order to secure your assistance in this matter, but you'll understand once Martin has explained everything. And I know that you and your wife are clever people, far cleverer than I could ever imagine being, but even you have to admit that Martin... I mean, he's an utter genius."

"I've known a few geniuses in my time," Jonathan replied, "and they all had one thing in common. They were all still of making great big crashing mistakes whenever their egos got the better of them!"

"Not Martin," she purred. "Martin's perfect in every way. When all of this is over he's going to love me forever and -"

"Love you?" he spat back at her, as if he

couldn't quite believe what he was hearing. "You poor deluded woman, what the hell are you talking about?"

"Martin adores me."

"Trust me," he replied, "you are *definitely* not Martin Delaney's type."

"You're just jealous that he's the one making this great discovery," she countered. "Why can't you be satisfied that you and your wife are essentially working as his assistants? I don't know much about the academic world, but that seems like a big privilege to me."

"Okay, I'm clearly not going to get any sense out of you," he replied, storming past her and heading up the stairs. "Where's Rebecca? Is she in the room?"

"I'm really not quite sure where she is right now," Ida said blankly, watching as he disappeared around the corner at the top of the staircase, then allowing herself a faint smile. "I think she might be taking a little rest."

***

"Rebecca?" Martin called out as he hurried along yet another corridor in the house's cold side, heading toward a pool of light spilling out from a doorway up ahead. "Rebecca, are you -"

As soon as he reached the doorway, he froze

as he saw the six skeletal children laid out on a set of tables. Falling completely silent, he stepped into the room and looked down at each of the corpses in turn as he made his way past them, and he began to realize that Martin Delaney's plan was far grander – yet far more grotesque – than he'd ever dared to imagine.

Reaching the farthest of the tables, he looked down at the body of a young girl. A few specks of flesh still clung to her skull, while her long hair had either been almost white all along or – perhaps more likely – had lost its color after decades in the darkness of a grave.

Holding a hand out, Martin was tempted to touch the corpse, hoping to find that she was simply a very detailed model. At the very last moment, however, he held back; somehow he could already tell that this was no facsimile, that this was in fact the dead body of one of the evacuated children who'd died many years earlier.

Over on the far side of the room, a floorboard creaked.

"Jonathan Pearson," Martin's voice said calmly. "Dear chap, it's so very good to see you again."

Slowly, Jonathan turned and saw his former colleague's beaming smile.

"I imagine," Martin continued, "that you have a great many questions."

"What the hell are you playing at?" Jonathan asked cautiously.

"I know, right?" Martin said. "Can you imagine what the university's ethics board would have to say about this? Old Prue Macauley'd be spitting feathers by now, and Howie Oakenshott's head would probably be spinning. That's the thing about a certain type of dusty old academic, isn't it? They just don't quite operate in the real world. No, that's not quite accurate... they don't *understand* the real world. They spend their entire lives working at the university, dreaming of making huge breakthroughs but never actually getting their hands dirty."

He stepped over to one of the corpses and reached out to touch the skull.

"But they never do anything worthwhile," he added softly, "because they can't see beyond the ends of their own noses."

"Why are you doing this, Martin?" Jonathan asked. "Have you lost your mind?"

"There's a ghost here," he replied, staring at the nearest corpse for a moment before looking up. "At least one. Of that I have absolutely no doubt. It took me a while to accept the truth, but Marlstone Hall is genuinely haunted. Don't ask me what that means for the rest of the world, because frankly I don't have a clue. But something's going on here and I mean to haul it out of the shadows and into the light."

"You're crazy," Jonathan told him.

At this, Martin merely chuckled.

"It's 2011," he pointed out. "I believe it's a tad politically incorrect to use mental health diagnoses as pejorative terms. Shame on you, Mr. Pearson."

"I mean it," Jonathan continued. "You faked your own death!"

"I spread some rumors," Martin countered. "I got my sister to help out. Of course, I never actually had her report my death to the authorities, so technically on paper I'm still very much alive. And in the furore that erupts once my discovery is made public, nobody's going to care too much about a few little white lies here and there. I needed to get you and your wife onboard with my work, and the best way to do that was by creating a narrative that you'd be unable to ignore."

"We came here because we heard it was the one case that you couldn't solve."

"Ta da," he replied dryly. "That part wasn't a lie."

"You could have just asked us to come."

He shook his head.

"No, that wouldn't have worked," he suggested. "I needed you to come here under your own steam. The whole idea was that I'd observe your investigation and use it as a kind of control group for the study. I needed to step out of the focal point and see what you and Rebecca achieved. Unfortunately things went a little wrong and you discovered the nature of my work too early, but that doesn't mean that we can't still achieve great things. I should have known that you'd see through little tricks like the ration card. I must admit, I made a mistake there. I didn't think to look up the details of when they were introduced."

He looked toward the doorway.

"Where's Ida?" he asked.

"I have no idea."

"Good," he continued, before stepping closer to Jonathan. "She's extremely weak-minded and easy to manipulate. A few promises of marriages here and a few touches in the right places and I had her wrapped around my little finger like... bacon on a sausage at Christmas. That's very important, because I needed to know from the start that I could get her to do anything I wanted. And so far that has turned out to be the case."

"Do you genuinely believe that the ghosts of these children are in the house?" Jonathan asked.

"The children?" He paused, before stepping around the nearest table and looking down at another of the corpses. "No, the children are merely the means to an end. I'm not sure that *they're* around. It was very convenient that they were buried here at Marlstone Hall, though. Grave-robbing wasn't exactly an enjoyable experience, but it was highly necessary. I must admit, at one point I believed that the children might be here, I even staged a little mock encounter with one to -"

Stopping suddenly, he looked at Jonathan again.

"Did you have a nice time visiting my sister, by the way?" he asked. "I'm assuming that young Katie gave you the folder, just as I asked her to?"

"So that was all lies too?"

"She was only too happy to oblige. All she needed in return was a gift card for some online music service."

"She was certainly convincing."

"I was trying to nudge you in the right direction," Martin told him. "To open your eyes. Tell me, did you recognize little Rose in that video? I disguised her very well, or at least I think I did."

"That was Rose?" Jonathan replied, thinking back to the image of the child in the video. Although he found it hard to believe, he could just about accept that Martin had achieved that particular deception. "No, I didn't recognize her at all."

"You were supposed to stumble into this moment all by yourself," Martin said firmly, "but as it is, now you get to play a more active role. We're going to capture indisputable evidence of the paranormal tonight, Jonathan. The ghost of Emma

Kemp has spent decades searching in vain for the children she let die." He gestured toward the bodies all around him. "Tonight... how can she resist finally coming for them?"

CHAPTER TWENTY-THREE

1939...

"MEREDITH, CAN YOU HEAR me?" Emma sobbed, placing a hand on one side of the young girl's face, waiting for even the faintest sign of life. "Meredith, please..."

Holding her breath, she watched the girl's features, but already she knew that she was too late. Just like the other five children, Meredith was gone now and her skin already felt so very clammy. Her slightly yellowing eyes were open, staring up at the ceiling, while her mouth remained frozen halfway through the prayer she'd been uttering in her final moments.

Slowly Emma reached over and closed the girl's eyes, and then she carefully folded the child's hands over one another on her chest.

"I see I'm too late," a voice barked from the doorway.

Turning, with tears running down her face, Emma saw that Dr. Crittenden had arrived from the village.

"That's six for six," Crittenden continued. "If you were a bowler, that would be an exceptional accomplishment. For a nurse trying to save the lives of her young charges, however, it's all rather lamentable."

"I tried," she stammered, getting to her feet. "Doctor, I don't know what went wrong. I did exactly what you told me to, I gave them the medicine exactly as you instructed me to but..."

Her voice trailed off and her words hung in the air, until slowly she looked down once more at poor Meredith Pool's corpse.

"I followed your orders so carefully," she whimpered.

"Evidently not," he replied, setting his case down before making his way over to the bed so that he too could observe the pitiful sight. "If you had followed my orders carefully, Nurse Kemp, at least five – and probably all six – of the children would still be alive. You must have fouled something up along the way."

"No, I swear," she said, shaking her head as more tears flowed freely down her cheeks.

"You can swear all you like," he sneered, "but the dead children are something of a giveaway. You and you alone have been responsible for their care here at Marlstone Hall, have you not?"

"Yes, but -"

"And I gave you very clear instructions."

"You did, truly you did, but -"

"Then what exactly do you think has happened here?" he snarled. "Woman, are you not capable of taking responsibility for your own actions? Even now, in the face of such tragedy, do you dare to profess that somebody else is to blame? Upon whose hands, if not your own, would you prefer to daub their blood?"

Turning to him, Emma opened her mouth to defend herself, but deep down she was already starting to understand that she *must* have made a mistake. After all, Dr. Crittenden had a fine reputation and had been a doctor for many years, whereas she was freshly out of training and had very little experience upon which to call. As much as she felt sure that she'd followed his instructions to a tee, now she understood that she simply must have made some kind of catastrophic mistake; a mistake, she realized with a growing sense of horror, that she could not even promise to avoid in the future. After all, how could she do so when she wasn't even sure what this mistake had been in the first place?

"So sad," Crittenden said, shaking his head as he walked away and picked up his case. "And very unnecessary. Those six children would have been better off left at their homes down south. They were whisked up here to keep them safe from German bombs, only to be murdered instead by English hands."

"I did my best," she said softly, unable to raise her voice above a whisper. "I did everything you told me to do."

"Evidently your best wasn't good enough," he said sternly. "Ms. Kemp, I shall do what I can do avoid too many questions being asked about this sorry incident. After all, there's no need to create yet more drama. I would advise you to do the same. There's no point telling too many people about your dismal failure here. Just take it on the chin, try not to think about it... and speak of it to nobody. Do you understand?"

Barely able to hear his words, Emma merely stared at the empty vials of medicine that she'd been using to treat the children.

"Good," Crittenden continued confidently, finally turning and walking out of the room. "That's the spirit. Onwards and upwards."

***

The muscle twitched slightly as the needle slid

through his skin, and a moment later a bony thumb pushed down on the plunger.

As soon as the medicine was in his veins, George Crittenden let out a sigh. He knew that the mixture hadn't been given enough time to work yet, but just knowing that it was in his body was enough. Sitting in a backroom at the village pub, he took a series of deep breaths before carefully sliding the needle out and setting it down.

"Foolish nurse," he muttered under his breath, thinking back to the sight of Nurse Kemp up at Marlstone Hall. "If she'd had her wits about her at all, she'd have realized that something wasn't working and she'd have diluted the medicine accordingly. It's really her fault entirely that those children perished."

Once he'd begun to feel the effect of the medicine coursing through his body, he got to his feet and began to tidy up. As soon as that was done, he took his case and headed to the door. He stopped and checked his reflection in the mirror, just to make sure that everything was alright, and then he pulled the door open and began to make his way through to the bar area.

As he did so, he realized that he could hear a great deal of animated chatter coming from the saloon area.

"Doctor Crittenden!" the landlord gasped as soon as he spotted him entering the room. "Have you heard?"

"I've heard a great many things today," Crittenden replied, "as I do every single day. I'm afraid you'll have to be rather more specific."

"That nurse up at Marlstone Hall," the landlord continued, as others gossiped all around the room. "Kemp or whatever her name was. She's only gone and hung herself!"

"Indeed," Crittenden said, showing no obvious sign of emotion at all. "That is... unfortunate news."

"How many children was it that died under her care again?" Alf Scrace asked from his spot on a nearby stool. "Six or seven, I heard."

"Six," Crittenden told him.

"Must've weighed heavy on her heart," Alf continued. "Then again, that'd be true of anyone, wouldn't it? I can't imagine how anyone could live with such guilt on their conscience."

"Quite," Crittenden said, checking his watch. "And now, gentlemen, if you'll excuse me I've got some more rounds to get through. It would seem that half the population of this parish has become bed-bound by one ailment or another. Heaven knows how we're going to win this war if everyone's so ill."

"No rest for the wicked, eh?" the landlord joked.

Once Crittenden was gone, the landlord got

back to work cleaning glasses, although after a moment he noticed that old Alf seemed troubled by something. Usually a very talkative fellow, Alf was now staring down at his pint of beer as if his mind was on some other matter entirely.

"Give over, Alf," the landlord said finally. "You're making me feel all queer sitting like that. What's wrong with you?"

"Nothing much," Alf replied, "but I can't help thinking about those children. I saw them when they arrived, you know. Bright young things, they were, and I remember thinking to myself that at least up here they'd be safe. And they *should* have been, too. I don't get it, though. That nurse seemed alright whenever I spoke to her, like her heart was truly in the right place. I can understand a mistake being made, p'raps, but not six times like this. And now to think that she's taken herself away with a noose."

He made the sign of the cross against his chest.

"Seven lives lost in such a short space of time," he continued. "It doesn't seem right to me. Not at all. And I'll tell you one thing for free. You wouldn't ever be able to persuade me to set food in that Marlstone Hall. Not now. Now with all the suffering there's been up there. Some kinds of suffering linger, and mark my words, there'll be plenty up at that place now. They oughta tear the place down, Sam. They oughtn't to let it still stand, not after all these terrible things have happened."

"Drink up, Alf," the landlord replied. "It's tragic what went on, but there's no point in you letting it get to you. Let's just hope they're all at peace now. That's the only saving grace about death, really. At least it ends all the suffering."

CHAPTER TWENTY-FOUR

Many years later...

"I NEED TO GO and find my wife," Jonathan Pearson said. "She must be -"

"Quiet!" Martin said as he flicked a switch on the wall, plunging the room into darkness. "I think she's close."

"Who is?" Jonathan asked.

"I told you. Emma Kemp, the nurse who was blamed for what happened to these children. Personally I'm convinced that the drug-addicted old doctor was responsible, but my understanding is that Emma never realized that. Overcome by a sense of guilt, she killed herself right here in the house. She put a rope around her neck and stepped off a chair, and that was the end of her. Or at least, she thought it would be the end of her, but something about true tragedy seems to positively breed the paranormal."

"I never thought I'd see the day," Jonathan replied, "when the great Martin Delaney lost his mind so thoroughly that he began to engage in... cheap parlor tricks."

"Just wait a few minutes and I'm sure you'll see," Martin said softly.

"I'm going to find Rebecca," Martin said, turning to leave, "and -"

Before he could finish, he heard a bumping sound coming from out in the corridor, followed by another. Footsteps were very slowly approaching the doorway, and although he instantly told himself that there was no reason to be concerned, he couldn't help but notice that these footsteps sounded very calm and very measured.

"It's her," Martin whispered.

Turning, Jonathan could just about see the other man's features picked out in the low moonlight that even now was streaming through a nearby window.

"I wanted you to be here to witness this," Martin continued. "The ghost of Emma Kemp has been trapped in this house ever since she died, constantly searching for the children but never able to find them. Tonight I have finally brought them to her and she won't be able to help herself. Sheer guilt will force her every step until she arrives, and then I -"

Grabbing his phone, he held it up and prepared to film the doorway.

"I developed a way of capturing them," he explained. "It's too complicated to explain now, but I'm certain that I'm about to capture the first verifiable footage of a ghost. This is going to change everything, Jonathan. Even you and Rebecca will have to admit that I'm right."

"I'll admit that you're crazy," Jonathan told him. "I'll admit that you've gone way too far."

"This is my life's work we're talking about," Martin replied, keeping the camera trained on the door as the footsteps made their way ever closer. "In a way, all my previous skepticism has been building up to this moment. Some people think that changing their mind is a sign of weakness, but to me it's the ultimate strength. To be able to follow the evidence, to be willing to break down one's own ego and accept that you were wrong... that's what marks a truly great mind."

"This isn't the work of a truly great mind," Jonathan insisted. "This is -"

"She's here!"

Jonathan opened his mouth to tell Martin once again that he was crazy, but at the last second he spotted movement over on the far side of the room. Turning, he spotted a figure moving through the darkness, slowly stepping through the doorway and approaching the tables. Although he was unable to make out the figure's features, something about the way she moved sent an immediate shiver down his spine.

"It's her," Martin continued with an awestruck smile as he kept his camera focused on the new arrival. "This is the ghost of Emma Kemp."

***

Slowly opening her eyes, Rebecca let out a slow groan as she felt a throbbing pain in the back of her head. Rolling over, she tried to get up, only to swiftly find that her body felt far too heavy. Blinking a couple of times in the darkness, she tried to work out what had happened, and finally she remembered her encounter outside with Ida Sinclair.

"We'll see about that," she'd said earlier, turning away from the crazed woman and tapping at her phone, determined to call for help. "I'm sorry, but I can't just stand by and watch as -"

And then...

And then something had slammed into the back of her head, and she understood now that she must have been knocked out cold.

Reaching up, she touched the sore spot and immediately winced. She couldn't feel any blood, however, so she figured that hopefully there wouldn't be any lasting damage. Still, as she finally managed to sit up, she found herself struggling to remember everything that had happened, and she still wasn't entirely certain what Ida had been up to, until suddenly she recalled the sight of Martin Delaney – very much alive – standing in one of the rooms, surrounded by the corpses of the children who'd died at Marlstone Hall all those years earlier.

Hauling herself up, and finding that she was still a little unsteady, she hurried to the door and tried to pull it open, only to find that it was locked.

"Help me!" she shouted, banging on the door for a moment before realizing that perhaps she shouldn't advertise the fact that she was awake.

Reaching into her pockets, she searched for her phone, only to find that it was missing. Figuring that Ida had taken it, she turned and looked around the room, and she spotted the displays that she'd seen earlier. Making her way over, she once again saw the images of herself and Jonathan. Evidently Martin Delaney had been planning to incorporate them into the insane story of Marlstone Hall. She still didn't quite understand how that was supposed to work, but all she knew in that moment was that she had to get away from the house and call for help.

Aware now that the door wasn't an option, she looked over at the only window in the room. Glancing around, she spotted a chair and pulled it over, hoping that she could use that to climb up. As she did so, however, she bumped against the display panels, knocking them down.

And then she froze as she saw the last panel, which until this moment had been hidden behind all the others.

"Arrogance or folly?" she read out loud, picking the panel up and seeing another photograph of herself and Jonathan. "Did the Pearsons die due to -"

Stopping herself just in time, she realized that this particular panel seemed to be the culmination of Martin and Ida's narrative about the house.

"Jonathan and Rebecca Pearson died here at Marlstone Hall," she read out loud, "because of their inability to recognize the truth. Until their final moments, they refused to believe in the house's secrets. And when they came face to face with the ghostly presence of Emma Kemp, they..."

Her voice trailed off for a moment as she understood exactly what Martin was planning.

"They chose death rather than enlightenment. Unwilling to embrace the truth, they chose instead to end their lives. And who's to say that their ghosts have not now been added to the corridors and rooms of Marlstone Hall? Are they now doomed to wander this place forever, as the perfect example of everything they believed to be impossible?"

"He's lost his mind," she whispered, taking a step back and letting the panel fall to the floor. "Someone has to stop him."

After pulling the chair all the way across the room, she climbed up and tried to reach the window, but she found that she was still a little too short. Once she'd made a few more fruitless attempts, she clambered back down and tried to come up with another plan. Her heart was racing and she knew she was running out of time, so finally she hurried back to the door and tried several times to smash it open.

"Damn it, Jonathan, where are you?" she hissed, wondering why her husband hadn't yet made it back from Sheffield to help. "I could really use you showing up right now. There's no need for -"

Suddenly hearing a clicking sound, she looked down at the lock. As the sound continued, she realized that someone was getting ready to open the door. Panicking, she rushed across the room and grabbed the chair, and then she held it up high above her head as she made her way back just as the door began to swing open. And then, at the very last second, just as she was about to slam the chair against her captor... she froze as she saw a terrified face staring up at her.

"Rose?" she stammered. "What are you doing here?"

"I think Mummy's in trouble," Rose said, and now her voice was trembling with fear. "I think she's done something really bad. Can you help her?"

CHAPTER TWENTY-FIVE

"WAIT!" MARTIN HISSED, REACHING out and putting a hand on Jonathan's arm to hold him back as the dark figure very slowly made its way past the various tables. "Isn't she beautiful? Isn't she the most magnificent thing you ever saw in your life?"

Wearing a black dress and with her face covered by a black veil, the figure continued to move slowly between the tables, stopping briefly at each of them as if she wanted to look one more time upon the faces of the dead children. With all the lights off, the figure was almost impossible to see, yet every so often she strayed into a patch of moonlight. Reaching out, she placed a pale hand on one of the corpses and hesitated for a moment, as if lost in a memory of everything that had happened many years earlier.

"This is ludicrous," Jonathan said after a moment. "I *know* that's Ida!"

"It's not Ida," Martin replied.

"Of course it is," Jonathan continued with a heavy sigh. "Do you seriously think that this is going to fool anyone? Emma Kemp was a nurse! Why would she be wearing a black cloak like... like some kind of widow in a horror movie?"

"There are still many mysteries when it comes to the dead," Martin said, before reaching out and gripping his arm as if to hold him back. "Don't let fear drive you to incorrect conclusions, Jonathan. If you try to talk to her, she'll undoubtedly leave us again and I might never be able to get her back. All my work would have been in vain. Please, just let this play out however the spirit of Emma Kemp prefers."

"You want me to humor you?"

"I want you to open your mind!" Martin said firmly.

"You're deluded," Jonathan replied, turning to him. "What kind of -"

Before he could finish, he spotted movement over at the door, and to his shock he saw Ida Sinclair stepping into the room. He stared at her for a moment before turning to look the other way, and now he saw that the ghostly figure had stopped at the far end of the room, seemingly facing the wall.

"Is that her?" Ida asked, clearly terrified as she backed away against the wall at the other end of the room. "Is... that the nurse?"

"I'm going to attempt to communicate with her," Martin explained. "All my research has suggested to me that this is possible. Jonathan, I know how this must be for you, but please just let me prove that I'm right. If I'm wrong, this will all fall apart very quickly anyway."

Jonathan opened his mouth to argue with him, to tell him that he was chasing shadows, but at the last second he realized that perhaps there was no point. He could see the madness in his former colleague's eyes and he knew that there was no point trying to reason with him, but a moment later Martin stepped aside and gestured toward the strange figure.

"Actually, Jonathan," he continued, "I've just had a much better idea. Why don't *you* make first contact with the spirit? After all, that seems like the best way to prove to you that this is real."

"You want *me* to talk to her?"

"Unless you're scared," Martin added with a faint, mischievous smile. "But why would you be scared? You're not actually starting to accept the truth, are you?"

"You and I have very different definitions of the truth," Jonathan told him as he realized that he really had no choice. He turned and looked at the figure – which he now assumed must be either an actress or some kind of hologram – and he told himself that the time had come to reveal whatever was really going on.

"I don't like this, Martin," Ida said. "I thought I was brave enough but now I'm not so sure."

"Of course you're brave enough," he told her. "Mr. Pearson here is the one who's going to make contact with the dead. And this room is already set up with multiple cameras that will capture everything." He patted the side of Jonathan's arm. "Well? What are you waiting for? There's no time like the present."

Figuring that this at least was true, Jonathan stepped past one of the tables and made his way closer to the figure, who remained at the far end of the room with her back turned. He could feel a tightening sense of dread in the pit of his stomach but he put that down to a very simple and very natural human reaction. Even the most logical of minds, he knew all too well, could occasionally be disturbed by well-planned tricks. And this particular trick, he reasoned, was actually being staged remarkably well.

As he made his way closer to the figure, however, he couldn't help glancing over his shoulder and seeing that both Martin and Ida were watching him very cautiously.

They really believe this crap, he told himself.

Looking at the figure again, he felt tempted to simply rush over and pull her hood back, but he told himself that he perhaps had to be a little smarter.

"Hello," he said finally, and he was very aware now of his voice breaking the moonlit silence of the room. "My name is Jonathan Pearson and I've been led to believe that you are the ghost of Emma Kemp, a nurse who died here many years ago. However, I know that isn't possible, so I'm going to give you one chance – and only one – to retain some integrity and come clean. Who are you really?"

He waited, but the figure kept her back to him. Glancing around, he saw no sign of a projector, so he figured that Martin had simply hired an actress. That in itself would be easy enough to set up – but also easy to uncover. There would be a paper trail for one thing, and for another any actress would likely not be so committed to the role; she'd be easy to break down, easy to press into a confession, and Jonathan told himself that Martin had slipped up.

And yet...

As he reached out to touch the figure's arm from behind, Jonathan couldn't help but notice that the air was becoming much colder.

"I know you're an actress," he said firmly, although he was disappointed to pick up a trace of doubt – perhaps even fear – in his own voice. "Or an accomplice of some kind. I know you're not a ghost."

Although part of him wanted to pull back, he forced himself to stay strong. After a moment longer he somehow found the strength to touch the figure's arm, but he immediately recoiled as he felt her icy flesh beneath the fabric.

"I know you are!" he snapped angrily, and now he knew he was starting to lose control. "Let's get this charade over with! Just admit the truth!"

Now he wanted to grab her, to force her to turn and perhaps even to rip the veil away from across her face. Failing that, he figured that he could simply step around her and confront her another way, yet something was holding him back.

As much as he told himself that this couldn't possibly be a ghost, on some deep physical level his body – his meat and bones and heart – seemed to be reacting in a very different way, as if they were picking up on warning signals that his brain was refusing to acknowledge.

"Just... the truth, damn it," he said, still trying to goad himself into seizing hold of the situation. "I know... I know you're not.... you're just..."

His voice trailed off, and after a moment the figure began to turn slightly, as if she was about to look at him. He caught sight of a hint of a profile beneath the veil, and in that instant he couldn't help himself.

For the first time in his life, terrified by the sight of an apparent ghost, Jonathan Pearson took a couple of involuntary steps back.

"Do you see now?" Martin called over to him. "Do you see the truth?"

He turned to Ida.

"He broke!" he exclaimed excitedly. "I broke him!"

"Stop it!" she sobbed, sinking down onto the floor as if she could no longer bear to witness something so horrifying. "Make it go away!"

Grabbing a knife from the counter, she held

it up.

"Don't let it come anywhere near me!"

"I'm glad you've finally come around to my way of thinking, Jonathan," Martin continued, making his way over and stopping to get a closer look at the figure. "Emma Kemp, my name is Martin Delaney and I wish to establish true first contact with a spirit from the spectral realm. You have no reason to fear me, I have merely brought the bodies of these children out so that you can be reunited with them. That's what you want, isn't it? And in return, I want your help. I want to finally prove that you and your kind are real."

"This can't be happening," Jonathan whispered. "It just can't..."

"Face me," Martin told the figure. "After all I've done, I need you to face me. I brought two independent witnesses here. The Pearsons were fully against my work until this moment. Now I need you to show me your face. You look almost exactly how I expected you to look, you're even wearing one of your old dresses, but it's your face I need to see as the ultimate proof."

He waited, yet the figure remained still, with its features only half turned to him and hidden beneath the veil.

"Show me your face!" Martin said again.

"It has to be a trick," Jonathan said under his breath as Ida continued to sob nearby. "A good trick, I'll grant you that, but some kind of -"

"Show me your face!" Martin shouted, suddenly stepping forward and grabbing the veil, quickly ripping it away. "I want -"

In that moment he froze as he saw a familiar face staring back at him. Jonathan froze too, momentarily unable to understand what was happening as he realized that the face of the spectral woman was also the face of his wife Rebecca.

CHAPTER TWENTY-SIX

Fifteen minutes earlier...

"I NEED YOU TO tell me exactly what's going on here," Rebecca said firmly, holding Rose's hand as she led the girl into the cold part of the house. "There's no more time for evasiveness. I need to know everything."

"Mr. Delaney came to look for ghosts."

"Yes, I understand that part."

"At first he said it was impossible. He was making fun of Mummy and I didn't like him. But then -"

After a few more paces, Rebecca turned and looked down at her.

"But then one night he changed," she continued, struggling to hold back tears. "He was really pale and he took Mummy away into another room, so that I wouldn't be able to hear. But I *could* hear, because I was naughty and I went to the other side of the door. I heard them talking."

"About what?"

"He said that there was a ghost here. Maybe more than one. He sounded really excited and he told Mummy that they had to be careful with who they told."

"So I was right," she replied. "He truly lost his mind."

"He told her that she couldn't tell anyone else," she explained, "and that he was going to stay for a few more days, and that then he was going to go away for a little while. He said he was going to come back, though, and then..."

Her voice trailed off for a moment, and she was clearly reluctant to continue.

"And then he kissed Mummy."

"That doesn't seem to be in character for Martin Delaney," she observed. "The man's always been famous for claiming that love doesn't even exist."

"He told her that they were going to do everything together," Rose went on. "Mummy... even asked him about me. She said that she had to be careful because of me, but he said he liked me and that he'd look after us both. And he said that Mummy would never have to worry about money again, because he'd marry her and they'd become rich as soon as people found out about the ghost here."

"He was pulling all the right strings to keep her under his control," Rebecca said ruefully.

"Then he started doing things in the garden," Rose said. "Mummy got angry at him for damaging the memorial and they had a big argument where he was shouting at her. Then he told her that she could get a new memorial if she wanted, but that it couldn't be put in place until he was sure he was done. And then I saw him dragging things into the house. I didn't realize at first that he'd dug up the children from the garden."

"He must have lost it completely," Rebecca said with a sigh. "He's suffering from some sort of psychotic break. I should have realized that from the moment he claimed that there were really ghosts here. Delusions are a classic symptom."

"He left for a while and then he came back," she continued. "He was different when he came back. He wasn't panicking as much. He kept telling Mummy that everything was going to be alright, and he even tried to be nice to me as well. But I was scared because I overheard him telling Mummy that he wanted to find all the ghosts. I see the other children sometimes, in the house, and I know they're hiding."

"Those are... not real," Rebecca explained.

"But I see them."

"That doesn't mean that they're real," Rebecca said firmly. "It means that you've got an impressionable young mind and you're being influenced by all of this. That's okay, though, because you're only young. In a way, it's the same thing that must have affected your mother. You want something to be real so much that eventually you start to see it."

"He made me dress up as a ghost," she admitted. "I didn't want to, but he said he needed to make a video to trick some other people into coming."

"That would be Jonathan and me," Rebecca said through gritted teeth. "He thought that if we saw the ghosts here, we'd make his work seem more legitimate. He planned this con very carefully."

"And then he made Mummy dress up too," she added, once again seemingly close to tears. "I think he wanted her to scare you."

"She didn't do a bad job," she muttered, thinking back to the sight of the ghostly woman in one of the rooms. "He has some items that Emma Kemp left behind. I remember him mentioning that. I'm betting the black dress is something she wore for the funeral of the children before..."

Her voice trailed off again.

"It might even have been the dress she was wearing when she killed herself. That was right *after* the funeral, wasn't it?"

"Are you mad at me?" Rose asked, sniffing back more tears. "Will Mummy be mad at me?"

"I'm not mad at you, and your mother won't be once she comes to her senses," Rebecca replied as she tried to figure out exactly how she was going to set everything straight. "But I think we need to shock her into that. Rose, we really don't have long. Do you happen to know where Martin Delaney and your mother have been keeping Emma Kemp's old possessions?"

***

"Looks like I was right," Rebecca said, standing in one of the offices and looking through some old photos that Martin had evidently collected. "I wish I hadn't been."

Several of the photos had clearly been taken in the immediate aftermath of Emma Kemp's suicide. A few showed her body on the floor after it had been cut down, while half a dozen showed different angles of her corpse hanging from the rafter; in a few, her horrified dead face could be seen, and in all the photographs she was wearing the same black dress that Rebecca had seen the supposed ghost wearing.

And the same black dress that was now hanging from a hook in the corner of the room.

"Some of this stuff must have been in the house for all this time," she said under her breath, before spotting some lights shifting in the next room.

Heading to an open doorway, she looked through and saw several laptops hooked up to monitors. She made her way over and found that the screens showed various views from different cameras, including a number in the room with the bodies of the children. A moment later she realized that some of the cameras showed Jonathan and Martin making their way through the house.

"He's back," she said, feeling a rush of relief for a few seconds, before that relief was tempered by a sense of concern. "But he's with Martin. He's in danger."

Having made her way to the door, Rose was about to ask a question when she was distracted by a shuffling sound. Turning, she looked back across the room just in time to spot a shadow moving in the corridor outside the room.

"I think it's time to play Martin Delaney at his own game," Rebecca said. "He's been treating us all like fools for long enough, and I'm including your mother in that. Rose, I'm going to go and take care of this once and for all, but I need you to stay here and be good. Can you do that?"

Still watching the corridor, Rose realized that she could hear whispered voices outside.

"Rose?"

Startled as a hand touched her shoulder, she spun around to see that Rebecca was towering above her.

"Rose, will you be okay here?" Rebecca continued. "I just need to know that you're safe."

Rose hesitated for a moment, before slowly nodding.

"Okay," Rebecca said, looking over at the black dress. "I'm worried that this might be the most idiotic plan ever, but I'm not sure that I can stomach another mind-bending conversation with that fool. If I want to get through to him properly, then I need to go down onto his level. I don't like that idea, but it'll only be for a few minutes and at least I should finally be able to nip all of this in the bud."

She still hesitated, wondering whether she was making a huge mistake, before rushing to the dress and taking it down from the hanger.

"Looks like it might even be almost the right size," she said, before starting to unbutton her own top. "Rose, this is going to seem very strange, but please don't judge me. The most important thing is that we sort all of this out tonight before it goes even further."

Barely even hearing those words, Rose was instead watching the open doorway. And although she told herself that there was probably nobody outside in the corridor, a few seconds later she heard some familiar whispering voices. In that moment she realized that she still needed to find some way to help the other children.

CHAPTER TWENTY-SEVEN

Several minutes later...

"REBECCA?" JONATHAN GASPED. "WHAT the hell are you doing?"

"Surprised to see me?" she replied, keeping her eyes fixed on Martin Delaney. "I thought you might be. After all, it's not every day that somebody plays you at your own game."

"You're supposed to be locked away," Martin sneered, before turning to Ida. "I told you to lock her away!" he shouted angrily, storming over to her. "Can't I rely on you for even the simplest of tasks?"

"I'm sorry!" Ida blurted out, sobbing on the floor. "Please don't be mad at me! I just want this to be over!"

"That's what we all want," Rebecca said calmly. "Martin, you used to be one of the finest minds I'd ever met. What went wrong?"

"Wrong?" he snapped, turning to her again. "I finally saw the truth... and you think that means something is wrong?"

"There's no ghost here," Rebecca told him. "Your videos were faked. All your so-called evidence is phony. You've got nothing but the same kind of pathetic trickery you used to expose."

"All of that was designed to get *you* to open your minds," he replied with the tense irritation of someone explaining things to a child. "I need a second opinion here, but I knew that you'd both arrive with closed, petty little minds. So I decided to nudge you along and make you at least consider other possibilities so that you'd be ready when the real ghost arrived."

He looked her up and down for a moment, clearly disgusted.

"Take that off," he snarled. "You're desecrating the memory of Emma Kemp."

"You've been doing that since the moment you turned this into such a circus," she replied. "For all your efforts, you still don't have one scrap of evidence that Emma Kemp's ghost is here at Marlstone Hall. All you've got is six dead children whose corpses you dug out of the ground. Is this really all worth it, Martin? Do you really think you'll make your fortune if you -"

"It's not about the money!" he screamed furiously, taking a step toward her. "It's about the honor!"

"There's no honor in what you're doing," she told him.

"Spoken like a true intellectual lightweight," he murmured, seething with rage. "I've spent my life disproving ghost stories. Do you think it's easy being so negative all the time? I conducted my research because I truly *wanted* to believe, yet at every juncture I was met with pathetic theatrics and overblown nonsense. Do you know how desperately I always wanted to step into one of those houses and find an actual ghost? I know you two enjoyed debunking these things, but for me it was something else. For me it was a search for proof that there's something else."

"You always warned against emotion in science," she told him. "Look at you now."

"When I came here, I finally found what I was looking for," he continued. "Or at least, the faintest tease of it. I realized that I had to lure the truth out, so I came up with a better plan."

"It was a ridiculous plan," Jonathan told him. "The old Martin Delaney, the Martin Delaney I got to know over the years, would never have done anything like this."

"The old Martin Delaney wasn't dying,"

Martin replied wearily. "The old Martin Delaney didn't have, at best, a couple of years left. The old Martin Delaney wasn't determined to finally prove that all his work has been worthwhile."

***

"Hello?"

Stopping in the doorway, Rose looked through into one of the old bedrooms. She felt sure that she'd followed the shuffling sound correctly, and she knew she'd seen the other children in this particular room at least once before, yet now there was no sign of them at all.

"I'm here," she continued, struggling to fight the urge to run away. "Mrs. Pearson told me to stay put, but I heard you and I... I knew I had to come and find you."

She waited, but deep down she knew that the children weren't supposed to be scary. After all, she'd seen glimpses of them several times before, so as she stepped into the room she felt sure that she was in no real danger. Glancing around, she watched the shadows and waited in case anything began to move, yet already she was starting to wonder whether she might have hit some kind of dead end, whether she'd taken a wrong turn somewhere or had followed the wrong sound.

And then, hearing a creaking sound, she

turned to see that a door in the far corner was slowly easing open to reveal the darkness beyond.

"Are you there?" she asked.

Silence.

Supposing that there was still no need to be scared, she began to make her way toward the open door. Looking through, she spotted a set of wooden steps leading down into what she assumed must be the basement of the building. Having never been down there much – and certainly not on her own – she hesitated as she realized that she should probably wait for an adult, but a few seconds later she heard the sound of footsteps running somewhere down below in a space at the bottom of the steps, almost as if the other children wanted to play.

"I'm not supposed to go down there," she called out.

Again, she heard no reply.

Only more footsteps, followed a few seconds later by a brief, echoing giggle.

"Can we play up here instead?" she asked, even though she already suspected that they weren't going to agree.

Making her way cautiously to the top of the wooden steps, she looked down and saw a bare stone floor far below. The air already seemed so much colder, but she'd noticed that phenomenon before and she knew it didn't necessarily mean that anything was wrong. And although she had no desire to go down into the house's basement, part of her still worried about the other children. After all, they seemed so lonely, and she knew from experience how that felt.

"Don't be scared," she said as she began to make her way down the wooden staircase, descending slowly into the chilly, slightly damp air below. "Everything's going to be okay. I think... I think Mrs. Pearson's going to put it all right. I think she knows what she's doing."

Reaching the bottom, she found that she could barely see at all. A shaft of light was breaking through a window high up on the far wall, picking out some kind of circular stone structure with a few broken wooden boards over the top. Having never been into this part of the house before, Rose was puzzled by the structure and as she made her way over she still had no idea what she was seeing. Finally she held her hands out and touched the wooden top, but she still found that this latest discovery made no sense.

"Are you here?" she said out loud.

She waited, but in the silence she heard nothing at all save – perhaps – for the faintest dripping sound.

"If you're not here, I'm going to go back upstairs," she continued, before turning and starting to head back to the staircase.

And then she froze as she heard a grinding sound, and she turned just in time to see that the boards were sliding off the stone circle. As those boards hit the ground, Rose realized that they'd exposed the top of what appeared to be some kind of old well. She vaguely remembered her mother mentioning a well in the house, and now – as she stared at the dark emptiness of its opening, she realized that she could hear a whispering sound coming from somewhere in the depths.

After looking around to make sure that there was no sign of anyone, she walked back over to the well. Standing on tiptoes, she found that she could just about see over the edge, although all she was able to make out now was absolute darkness. She blinked a few times, waiting in case her eyesight became a little better, but she still saw nothing. At the same time, she could hear several voices whispering in the void below, and she felt that she just about recognized them as the same voices she'd heard several times in the house.

"Why are you down there?" she asked.

Hearing more whispers, she began to wonder whether a voice was trying to tell her something. She leaned a little further over the edge, trying in vain to make out the words, and now her toes were on the verge of lifting up off the ground. Finally she leaned even further, until she was staring down directly into the darkness, but still the voices refused to quite become clear.

"I can't hear you," she said, unable to hide a sense of frustration. "I think... I think I'd better go upstairs and fetch Mrs. Pearson. She'll know what to do."

With that, she turned to leave. At the last second, however, a rotten hand reached up and grabbed her arm, pulling her hard. She barely had time to cry out as she tumbled into the darkness and disappeared into the depths of the well.

CHAPTER TWENTY-EIGHT

"I SHOULD GO AND find Rose," Ida whimpered, slowly hauling herself up off the floor as she sniffed back more tears. "She might -"

"You're not going anywhere," Martin sneered, turning to her.

"But -"

"Stay right there!" he snapped angrily. "You've already caused me enough problems! I thought I could rely on you, I'd thought I'd managed to get through to you! I suppose I should have known that you'd turn out to be just as stupid as you look. Maybe even worse."

"But -"

"Will you just shut up?" he shouted. "You stupid bitch, for once in your life can't you just leave me alone?"

"I'm sorry," she sobbed, before pausing for a moment. "But you're still going to marry me, aren't you? And we're still going to be rich? You promised, Martin."

"I'll get to you later," he said darkly, before turning to Rebecca again. "You've made a mockery of this entire process. I invited you here to become part of a great scientific study, and how do you repay me? By interfering and getting in my way."

"I saw the last panels you had made up," she told him. "The ones that claim Jonathan and I died here."

"Those were just for Ida's sake," he said with a sigh. "Don't you get it yet? I told her we'd turn Marlstone Hall into some great museum about the paranormal, but that was just to get her on my side. I filled her head with all sorts of dreams so that she'd let me get my work done, but none of that matters now. We're so close to finding the proof we need, and with your help I can get over the last little hurdle."

He waited for a reply, before turning to Jonathan.

"At least *you* get it, don't you?" he continued. "Tell your wife to pipe down so we can work. We'll put this pathetic little display behind us and get on with the business of luring the ghost of Emma Kemp back out, and then we'll have all the proof we need."

"You were never going to marry me?" Ida cried, staring at the back of his head.

"Jonathan, you and I can achieve great things," Martin explained, ignoring Ida completely now. "Everything is perfectly set up. Perhaps your wife is a little histrionic, but I know you have a good mind. You won't let emotion get the better of you. By the time the sun comes up, we can have all the proof we need. Obviously I'll be credited as the leader of this project, it'll be my lasting legacy, but as one of my key assistants you'll still be lauded. Hell, I foresee a trip to the Nobel Institute for both of us if this all goes well."

"You've become everything you always professed to hate," Jonathan replied. "Everything you always railed against."

"You're letting emotion cloud your judgment," Martin told him. "Fear. Embarrassment. Pride. You're letting all these things stop you seeing the truth, which is that we stand on the brink of a great discovery. And when we're done here -"

"*I'm* the one letting emotion take over?" Jonathan said, clearly aghast at this suggestion. "I'm not the one who's been faking ghosts on camera and going to ridiculous lengths to pull off some kind of stunt! Martin, if anyone here is letting emotion run roughshod over scientific rigor, it's you!"

"Nonsense!" Martin shouted angrily. "There's no room for emotion in my study! Only -"

Suddenly he let out a shocked gasp and froze. Behind him, Ida grabbed him by the shoulder to hold him still, and a moment later Martin gasped again as if he was trying but failing to get any words out.

"You told me you loved me," Ida sobbed, as Martin slowly dropped to his knees. "You told me you were going to marry me, and that we'd be rich. But it was all a lie, wasn't it? You're just like all the rest! You promise and promise and promise, but in the end you all leave. Either you die or you run off or you find some other excuse, but you always go away and leave me all alone! Why can't I just have one person in the whole world who's mine?"

Martin tried once more to speak, but already a trickle of blood was running from one corner of his mouth. He looked at Jonathan, as if begging for help, before finally toppling forward and landing dead with his face against the floor. A large knife was protruding from his back, and as she stepped away Ida looked down at the blood on her right hand.

"What the hell did you do?" Jonathan shouted, racing over and pulling her away.

Hurrying across the room, Rebecca dropped to her knees and began to check Martin's body for any sign of a pulse. After a few frantic attempts, however, she pulled back as she saw his dead eyes staring up at her.

"He promised he was going to take care of me!" Ida sobbed, crumpling down onto the floor as tears streamed down her face. "He said we were going to stay here forever and be happy!"

***

"I found finally a phone that's connected to the landline," Jonathan said a few minutes later as he hurried back into the room. "The police and an ambulance crew are on their way."

Still in a heap on the floor, Ida was sobbing gently and whispering to herself.

"I think she's suffering from a complete breakdown," Rebecca said softly, still wearing the black dress. "She'd pinned all her hopes to the dreams Martin Delaney offered her. When she heard the truth, she couldn't handle it."

"So much for keeping emotion out of science," he suggested.

"You can't keep emotion out of anything," she countered. "And I don't think you should. But you can keep it in check, and you can stop it destroying everything. Isn't that the very definition of growing up?"

As those words left her lips, she spotted Martin's corpse on the floor.

"In theory, at least. I just can't believe that the great Martin Delaney could have allowed himself to fall so far. How are we even going to begin to explain any of this when the police arrive?"

"Fortunately it looks like he documented his work extensively," he replied. "From what I can tell, everything should have been caught on camera from multiple angles. And I haven't even looked at his paperwork yet, but I'm sure there'll be even more laid out in there. Which is bloody good luck, frankly, because I'm not sure that anyone would have believed us if we didn't have any firm proof."

"I'd like to get a copy of some of that stuff before we leave," she told him. "And before the police arrive, preferably. Just so we can study it all properly."

"I'll get onto that," he replied. "Will you be okay waiting in here until help shows up?"

"I don't think Ida's going to be much of a threat to anyone now," she suggested. "The poor woman must have been at the end of her tether. Not that desperation is any excuse for murder, of course, but I'm pretty sure that Martin played with her emotions so much that she could no longer control herself. I wonder what'll happen to -"

Stopping suddenly, she looked around the room.

"Jonathan, have you seen Rose anywhere?"

"No," he replied, stopping in the doorway and turning to her. "Isn't she in bed?"

"I told her to stay put in the office," she said

cautiously, "but... she really doesn't strike me as the kind of girl to stay put anywhere. She's got the same slightly rebellious streak as Alicia."

"Then she could be anywhere."

"Do you think she saw what just happened?"

"She might have done, but there was no sign of her."

"Then where exactly did she go?"

"I'm sure she's around," Jonathan suggested, checking his watch. "I'd better go and look for those videos before they disappear into -"

"Something's wrong," she said firmly, unable to shake a sense of unease. "Call me crazy but I can feel it in my bones somehow. There's no way a girl like Rose Sinclair would simply wander off while all of this is going on. She'd either be here or..."

Her voice trailed off for a few seconds as she tried to make sense of something that was bubbling away in the back of her mind. As much as she told herself that she had no reason to be concerned, Rose's sudden disappearance still made absolutely no sense whatsoever, and as she stepped over to the doorway and looked out into the corridor she couldn't shake the worry that somehow the girl might have managed to get herself into trouble again.

"What's wrong?" Jonathan asked. "Did you

hear something?"

"Absolutely nothing at all," she replied cautiously. "And that's what's worrying me. Where did she go?"

CHAPTER TWENTY-NINE

"ROSE?" REBECCA CALLED OUT as she hurried into yet another room, having spent the past few minutes searching for the girl. "Rose, can you hear me?"

She waited, but still the only response was silence. Marlstone Hall was huge, she knew that, and the odds of finding one person in so many rooms and corridors seemed low, especially when that person was perhaps trying to hide. At the same time, Rebecca still couldn't quite rid herself of the sense that something more serious was wrong, that somehow she was picking up on a sense of dread.

She knew that any talk of 'senses' or 'picking up' was crazily unscientific, of course, but in that moment she simply couldn't help herself.

"Rose, it's okay," she said cautiously, feeling

as if she might be getting closer. "I understand that you might be scared, but things are going to start getting better now. Your mother..."

As her voice faded to nothing, she realized that there was no good way to explain the fact that Rose's mother had murdered Martin Delaney. Sure, a defense of diminished responsibility would probably be quite easy to put forward, but there was no escaping the fact that Ida Sinclair was now facing significant time in – at the very least – some kind of psychiatric hospital. And if Rose knew that, then after years of isolation at the house she would almost certainly be terrified of the outside world.

"Rose," she continued, still unable to shake the feeling that she was getting closer as she stepped into the room. A floorboard shifted slightly and groaned beneath her left foot. "It's me. Can we at least talk?"

She saw a closed door on the other side of the room, but there was nothing to suggest that Rose had recently passed this way. Nothing, that is, except a niggling sense of concern in the pit of Rebecca's belly.

"It's hopeless," she said finally, turning to head back into the corridor. "There's no -"

Stopping suddenly, she looked at the closed door again. Based on her admittedly ropy understanding of the house's layout, she felt sure that this particular door shouldn't really lead anywhere, at least not to a proper room. She knew that there was an old study on the other side of one wall and that the other wall bordered the garden, so she found herself wondering exactly where that door could lead. And although she knew she had to keep searching for Rose, after a few seconds she began to make her way over.

"She's ours!"

Startled, she turned and saw a young girl standing in the open doorway behind her.

"Let her stay with us," the girl begged, with tears in her eyes. "We just want another friend!"

"Who the -"

Before she could finish, Rebecca saw the girl racing away out of sight. She hurried to the doorway and looked out into the corridor, but already the girl was gone.

"Who are you?" she asked, raising her voice a little. "Hello? Please come back, I just want to talk to you!"

Her heart was pounding, but as the seconds passed she realized that the girl was well and truly gone. She still had absolutely no idea who she might have been, yet she couldn't help but note that she'd been wearing decidedly old-fashioned clothing, as if she'd been dressed up to *look* like someone from many decades earlier.

From around the time of the Second World War, perhaps.

Taking a step forward, she was about to set off in pursuit of the girl when she stopped again. Turning, she looked at the closed door in the corner of the room and realized that the girl had almost seemed to be trying to lure her away from that spot. Although she still wasn't entirely sure what was happening, she found herself once again pondering that door and wondering exactly what might be behind it.

And that crazy sense of dread was still gnawing away inside her gut.

Heading back across the room, she grabbed the handle and pulled the door open. On the other side, a set of wooden steps led down beneath the house into what she could only assume must be the basement.

"Rose?" she called out, wondering whether her gut was trying to tell her something. "Rose, are you down there? Rose, if you are, can you please come up? We... we need to talk about something important. I need to tell you something about your mother."

Hearing only silence, she wondered whether she should go and check. Just as she was about to walk away, however, she realized that she could hear the faintest splashing sound coming from somewhere deep in the depths of the house.

"Rose?" she said cautiously, starting to make her way down the wooden steps. "Are you there?"

The splashing sound stopped, and Rebecca stopped too – just a few steps down toward the basement.

"Rose?" she whispered.

After a few seconds, realizing that she was in danger of getting distracted, she turned and headed back up. She knew there was no reason why Rose would have gone down into the house's basement and – besides – she told herself that she had to track down the strange little girl. As she reached the top and swung the door shut, she figured that Marlstone Hall still had a few surprises left to reveal.

***

"Help me!" Rose gasped, finally bursting up from beneath the cold, dirty water and grabbing a metal plate on the well's stone wall. "Please!"

Desperately trying to get her breath back, with water already up to her neck, she gripped the plate as hard as she could manage. Since being dragged down, she'd been constantly struggling to stay above the waterline, with hands reaching up from the depths and trying to pull her back underwater.

"Mummy!" she shouted, barely able to get any words out at all. "Mrs. Pearson, please -"

Before she could finish, she felt another small hand grabbing her ankle and pulling hard. This time she was able to hold herself up by hanging on the plate, but her fingers were already starting to slip and she knew she didn't have long. Having fought her way to the surface so many times already, now she felt as if she was becoming too weak. Her arms and legs were burning with pain and she felt certain that this might be her last chance to get to freedom.

Looking up, she was just about able to make out the wet stones glinting above. She spotted another metal plate a little higher up, so she started to climb, just about managing to find gaps in the stonework that allowed her to haul herself up. Slipping free of the hand on her ankle, she finally pulled herself above the water – only for two more hands to grab her from below. This time the hands were too strong and she could already feel herself getting dragged back down.

"Help!" she screamed. "I'm down here!"

"We want you to stay with us," a boy's voice growled from the depths. "It's been so long since we had a new friend. Why don't you want to stay and play with us?"

"Make her stay," a girl added. "Please make her play."

"Help me!" Rose shouted at the top of her voice. "Please!"

"You'll like it once you're here with us," another boy hissed. "We promise. And we can all play forever!"

Reaching up, Rose tried to pull herself to the next metal plate, but in that moment she began to slip. Letting out another cry, she just about managed to steady herself, but already she could feel more hands clawing at her body and trying to drag her deeper and deeper down. And this time, on the verge of passing out, she realized that she could no longer fight back. Instead she could only reach up with one trembling arm as she desperately tried to find some way to pull herself to safety, even as the hands dragged her deeper down into the water.

"Rose!"

Suddenly another, larger hand grabbed hers and pulled, lifting her out of the foul-smelling water. Barely able to understand what was happening, Rose felt another arm wrapping around her waste before she was hauled up higher, and eventually she was sent tumbling over the top of the well until she slammed down against the rough floor.

"Rose, what happened?" Rebecca gasped frantically, kneeling next to her and checking her for cuts or other injuries. "What were you doing in there?"

For a moment Rose could only stare up at her, before turning and looking at the well again.

She thought of the hands down at the bottom that had been pulling at her body, but she told herself that she was safe now. A moment later she turned and grabbed Rebecca, shivering wildly and clinging to her tight.

"It's okay," Rebecca said, holding her firmly. "It's a miracle I came back down. At the last second I just... I knew somehow that you were down here."

"Don't let them get me!" Rose sobbed frantically as she felt fear flooding through her body. "Please, Mrs. Pearson! Keep them away from me! Don't let them pull me back down!"

CHAPTER THIRTY

"MRS. SINCLAIR WILL BE taken for an initial assessment at Adenbrooke's," the officer said as morning light began to creep across the lawn in front of Marlstone Hall, "and young Rose will be looked after be specialist officers."

"Where will she go?" Rose asked. "Who's her next of kin?"

"We're trying to establish that," the officer continued, "but it's not easy. As far as we can tell, her aunt's the only family she had left."

"Her aunt?"

"Mrs. Sinclair."

"You mean..."

Rebecca hesitated for a moment as she tried to understand exactly what he meant.

"I thought Ida was Rose's mother," she said

finally.

"Yes, that seems to be the impression she gave a lot of people," the officer replied, rolling his eyes. "Even young Rose believed it. But we've established that Rose's mother was actually a woman named Cathy Radcliffe who died shortly after giving birth. The father was dead too, along with the grandparents, so Cathy's sister Ida took her in. She never actually formally adopted her, though. As it turns out, Rose Sinclair's actual legal name is Rose Radcliffe."

"I had no idea," Rebecca admitted, before spotting Rose being helped into a police car. "I'd like to talk to her, if that's alright."

"I'm afraid that won't be possible right now," the officer said. "She's a very vulnerable child and the attending team's initial assessment is that she's extremely traumatized. She kept talking about ghost children in a well. Do you know anything about that?"

"I mentioned it in my statement," Rebecca told him. "The other officer took it down."

"We'll need you to give a fuller statement in due course," he explained. "First, though, we need to review the material inside the house. I'm not doubting you for one second, Mrs. Pearson, but the story you and your husband gave us seems a little... convoluted. I'm sure you'll understand that we need to go through the footage, in particular, to make sure that everything matches up."

"Of course," Rebecca said as Jonathan made his way over. "If there's anything else we can do, just let us know."

"I got as much as I could," Jonathan whispered, quickly showing her a flash drive before slipping it back into his pocket. "I can't quite believe that I'm at the stage now where I'm stealing evidence from a crime scene, but I guess that's just the mess we're in. At least those tapes are also on the main system. No-one's going to accuse us of anything."

Rebecca watched as the car containing Rose was driven away, and then she turned to look at the house.

"Did they find the other girl?" she asked.

"Rebecca -"

"I know, I know," she continued, "you think that I was just stressed. And you might well be right, but I saw her so clearly. And she looked just like one of the evacuees in the photograph. Don't worry, I'm not saying that I saw a ghost, but I saw *something*. And then there's the fact that I somehow knew Rose was in that well. I can't explain it, but on some instinctual level... I just knew."

"We should get going," he replied, placing a hand on her shoulder. "Our last haunted house case has turned out to be by far the most memorable, and we're going to face a barrage of questions about

Martin Delaney when we get home. We should probably figure out what we're going to say. I vote for keeping it simple."

"We'll just say that he lost his mind," she suggested, "and -"

In that moment she spotted movement reflected in one of the windows of the house. She saw a woman walking across the lawn, surrounded by six children. Turning, she looked at the lawn and saw no-one. When she looked at the window again, the sight was already gone, but for a moment it had seemed so real.

"Rebecca?"

"You're right, let's get out of here," she replied, turning to him again as a shiver ran through her bones. "I know I probably shouldn't admit this, Jonathan, but... Marlstone Hall has managed to get to me a little. More than any of the other houses we've been to. I just can't quite believe how bad things got here."

***

One month later, sitting at the dining room table, Rebecca once again watched the video of a ghostly boy at Marlstone Hall. At least, that was what the video *purported* to show, but it had long been clear that in fact Martin Delaney had merely dressed Rose up and had tried to pass her off as a ghost.

Something about the video was troubling Rebecca, however, even if she couldn't quite put her finger on the precise nature of the problem.

"Coming to bed?" Jonathan asked wearily, stopping in the doorway.

"Soon," she murmured, rewinding the video and watching it again.

"You've been sitting there for hours," he pointed out. "Rebecca, you'll drive yourself crazy. And you haven't forgotten that you've got *actual* work to do tomorrow, have you?"

"Of course I haven't," she replied, turning to him. "I just want to check a few more things."

"Well, I'm turning in," he muttered. "Sleep well when you eventually come up."

"Jonathan?"

He looked back at her.

"I spoke to someone at the station today," she continued, having spent several hours wondering exactly how to broach this subject, "and he told me... I know I shouldn't care, but apparently Rose is going to be sent to some kind of home for orphaned children."

"That's probably the best place for her."

"Is it?"

"Where would you suggest instead?"

He waited for an answer, before letting out a sigh.

"We have a spare room," she said firmly,

having anticipated his resistance, "and financially it's not a problem. We both have good jobs, we're respected members of the community and we already have a daughter of our own. In many ways this would be an ideal home for -"

"You want to adopt Rose Sinclair?"

"Radcliffe," she replied softly. "It's Rose Radcliffe, remember?"

"Whatever it is," he continued, "I really don't think we're in any position to go around adopting stray little girls."

"It's only one little girl," she pointed out, "and I really started to like her. Besides, we wouldn't necessarily have to go through the whole adoption process. I spoke to someone today who said we can simply foster her for a while."

"Rebecca, I don't know..."

"Can we at least consider the possibility?" she asked. "Can we look into it and see how feasible it might be?"

"How would Alicia feel?"

"I'll talk to her. I'll make her understand."

He hesitated, but deep down he knew that there was usually no point going against his wife's wishes.

"We'll think about it," he said finally. "That's all I'm willing to commit at the moment. Now, you might have infinite energy for staying up, but I need to get my beauty sleep."

As her husband headed upstairs, Rebecca was left looking once more at her laptop's screen. She knew full well that she needed to get some rest, yet at the same time this particular video was nagging at her. She set it playing again, watching as Rose – dressed up as a ghostly young boy – once again appeared on the screen. Once the video was over she realized that she'd exhausted this line of investigation, yet she quickly found herself playing it yet again. Somehow, deep down, part of her remained convinced that she was missing something.

And then, on what she must have been her hundredth viewing of the video, she suddenly saw something in the back of the image.

Hitting a button to freeze the video, she had to rewind several frames before finally she spotted the faintest hint of a pale face in the gloom. She told herself that she had to be wrong, yet she couldn't help wondering whether somebody had been watching Rose and Martin during their little filming session, and she also couldn't help thinking that this extra face looked a lot like the strange girl she'd briefly encountered at Marlstone Hall.

"You were tired," Jonathan had told her several times. "You imagined it. What other possible explanation could there be?"

Still staring at the vague, smudged image, she told herself that her husband was right, that there had been no actual ghosts at the house. At the same time, she thought back to the sight of a woman leading some children away, and she thought too of Rose's babbled claims about hands in the well.

As the clock ticked past midnight, she watched the video again – then again, and again and again for another couple of hours. And each time, as she briefly saw the spectral face in the background, she found herself wondering whether Martin Delaney might just have caught some evidence of the supernatural after all. She couldn't quite come up with an answer, however, even as she watched the video again.

And again.

And again and again and again and again and again...

Next in this series

The Haunting of Lotham Lodge
(The Ghosts of Rose Radcliffe book 3)

After their terrifying experience at Marlstone Hall, everything has changed for Rebecca and Jonathan Pearson. They still want to find proof of the paranormal, however, so they quickly accept an offer to explore the mysterious Lotham Lodge in West Sussex.

As soon as they arrive at the house, they realize that something is very wrong. The lodge's sole occupant seems to have lost his mind, yet others appear to want to keep him in place. Strange whispers are heard at night and locals from the nearby village insist that a sinister force lurks in the shadows.

Soon Rebecca and Jonathan find themselves being pushed to the edge of their beliefs and beyond. For Jonathan, however, the situation at Lotham Lodge soon turns out to be highly personal. When the past comes bursting into the present, can even the most logical mind survive?

Also by Amy Cross

1689
(The Haunting of Hadlow House book 1)

All Richard Hadlow wants is a happy family and a peaceful home. Having built the perfect house deep in the Kent countryside, now all he needs is a wife. He's about to discover, however, that even the most perfectly-laid plans can go horribly and tragically wrong.

The year is 1689 and England is in the grip of turmoil. A pretender is trying to take the throne, but Richard has no interest in the affairs of his country. He only cares about finding the perfect wife and giving her a perfect life. But someone – or something – at his newly-built house has other ideas. Is Richard's new life about to be destroyed forever?

Hadlow House is brand new, but already there are strange whispers in the corridors and unexplained noises at night. Has Richard been unlucky, is his new wife simply imagining things, or is a dark secret from the past about to rise up and deliver Richard's worst nightmare? Who wins when the past and the present collide?

Also by Amy Cross

If You Didn't Like Me Then, You Probably Won't Like Me Now

One year ago, Sheryl and her friends did something bad. Really bad. They ritually humiliated local girl Rachel Ritter, before posting the video online for all to see. After that night, Rachel left town and was never seen again. Until now.

Late one night, Sheryl and her friends realize that Rachel's back. At first they think there's on reason to be concerned, but a series of strange events soon convince them that they need to be worried. On the outside, Rachel acts as if all is forgiven, but she's hiding a shocking secret that soon starts to have deadly consequences.

By the time they understand the full horror of Rachel's plans, Sheryl and her friends might be too late to save themselves. Is Rachel really out for revenge? What does she have in store for her tormentors? And just how far is she willing to go? Would she, for example, do something that nobody in all of human history has ever managed to achieve?

If You Didn't Like Me Then, You Probably Won't Like Me Now is a horror novel about the surprising nature of revenge, about the power of hatred, and about the future of humanity.

Also by Amy Cross

The Soul Auction

"I saw a woman on the beach. I watched her face a demon."

Thirty years after her mother's death, Alice Ashcroft is drawn back to the coastal English town of Curridge. Somebody in Curridge has been reviewing Alice's novels online, and in those reviews there have been tantalizing hints at a hidden truth. A truth that seems to be linked to her dead mother.

"Thirty years ago, there was a soul auction."

Once she reaches Curridge, Alice finds strange things happening all around her. Something attacks her car. A figure watches her on the beach at night. And when she tries to find the person who has been reviewing her books, she makes a horrific discovery.

What really happened to Alice's mother thirty years ago? Who was she talking to, just moments before dropping dead on the beach? What caused a huge rockfall that nearly tore a nearby cliff-face in half? And what sinister presence is lurking in the grounds of the local church?

Also by Amy Cross

American Coven

He kidnapped three women and held them in his basement. He thought they couldn't fight back. He was wrong...

Snatched from the street near her home, Holly Carter is taken to a rural house and thrown down into a stone basement. She meets two other women who have also been kidnapped, and soon Holly learns about the horrific rituals that take place in the house. Eventually, she's called upstairs to take her place in the ice bath.

As her nightmare continues, however, Holly learns about a mysterious power that exists in the basement, and which the three women might be able to harness. When they finally manage to get through the metal door, however, the women have no idea that their fight for freedom is going to stretch out for more than a decade, or that it will culminate in a final, devastating demonstration of their new-found powers.

AMY CROSS

Also by Amy Cross

The Ash House

Why would anyone ever return to a haunted house?

For Diane Mercer the answer is simple. She's dying of cancer, and she wants to know once and for all whether ghosts are real.

Heading home with her young son, Diane is determined to find out whether the stories are real. After all, everyone else claimed to see and hear strange things in the house over the years. Everyone except Diane had some kind of experience in the house, or in the little ash house in the yard.

As Diane explores the house where she grew up, however, her son is exploring the yard and the forest. And while his mother might be struggling to come to terms with her own impending death, Daniel Mercer is puzzled by fleeting appearances of a strange little girl who seems drawn to the ash house, and by strange, rasping coughs that he keeps hearing at night.

The Ash House is a horror novel about a woman who desperately wants to know what will happen to her when she dies, and about a boy who uncovers the shocking truth about a young girl's murder.

Also by Amy Cross

Haunted

Twenty years ago, the ghost of a dead little girl drove
Sheriff Michael Blaine to his death.

Now, that same ghost is coming for his daughter.

Returning to the small town where she grew up, Alex
Roberts is determined to live a normal, quiet life. For the
residents of Railham, however, she's an unwelcome
reminder of the town's darkest hour.

Twenty years ago, nine-year-old Mo Garvey was found
brutally murdered in a nearby forest. Everyone thinks
that Alex's father was responsible, but if the killer was
brought to justice, why is the ghost of Mo Garvey still
after revenge?

And how far will the real killer go to protect his secret,
when Alex starts getting closer to the truth?

Haunted is a horror novel about a woman who has to
face her past, about a town that would rather forget, and
about a little girl who refuses to let death stand in her
way.

AMY CROSS

Also by Amy Cross

The Curse of Wetherley House

"If you walk through that door, Evil Mary will get you."

When she agrees to visit a supposedly haunted house with an old friend, Rosie assumes she'll encounter nothing more scary than a few creaks and bumps in the night. Even the legend of Evil Mary doesn't put her off. After all, she knows ghosts aren't real. But when Mary makes her first appearance, Rosie realizes she might already be trapped.

For more than a century, Wetherley House has been cursed. A horrific encounter on a remote road in the late 1800's has already caused a chain of misery and pain for all those who live at the house. Wetherley House was abandoned long ago, after a terrible discovery in the basement, something has remained undetected within its room. And even the local children know that Evil Mary waits in the house for anyone foolish enough to walk through the front door.

Before long, Rosie realizes that her entire life has been defined by the spirit of a woman who died in agony. Can she become the first person to escape Evil Mary, or will she fall victim to the same fate as the house's other occupants?

AMY CROSS

Also by Amy Cross

The Haunting of Quist House
(The Ghosts of Rose Radcliffe book 1)

She wakes up alone in a dark house. She has no memory, no idea who she is or where she came from. Blood runs from a wound on one side of her head. She hears strange sounds coming from one of the rooms upstairs. She still doesn't remember anything, but she's starting to realize the awful truth.

She's trapped inside a haunted house.

Not even knowing her own name, the woman starts searching for clues. The strange sounds continue. Is she truly alone, or are there others in the house? And if there are others, are they friend or foe? After making her first shocking discovery, the woman begins to fear the worst. Time is running out. The doors and windows are sealed shut. Nothing makes sense, but a grandfather clock in the hallway seems to offer clues.

Who is this woman? What was she doing in the house before she lost her memory? And even if she remembers in time, will she be able to stop the evil that lurks in the shadows?

AMY CROSS

Also by Amy Cross

The Haunting of Saward Island

Trying to fix their damaged boat, Jacqui Sinclair and her family stop at a remote island that doesn't appear on any maps. They soon discover the horrifying secret that caused previous generations to hide the island's existence from the rest of the world.

Many years ago, the island was the scene of an unspeakable tragedy. Ever since, a malevolent spirit has been lurking in the long grass, waiting near a bare wooden cross for its chance to gain revenge. For Jacqui and the others, their only hope lies in deciphering the clues left behind at a remote lighthouse, where a skeleton crew once tried and failed to defeat the same evil force.

If they fail, the Sinclairs will meet the same grisly fate that has befallen all those who have made the fatal mistake of setting foot on Saward Island...

AMY CROSS

Also by Amy Cross

13 Nights in Crowford

A murdered woman lingers in the old school, waiting for someone to uncover the identity of her killer. A dying painter arrives in the town and finds himself drawn into a nun's final mission. A hunted man takes refuge in an old seaside hotel but finds more than he bargained for. A man returns home after the war, but what dark secret is he hiding?

On the southern coast of England, the town of Crowford has long had a reputation for ghosts. Some even say that the town is home to more ghosts than people. Almost every part of Crowford is haunted, and to prove that claim, here are thirteen stories about the town's mysterious past – from the days before the town had even been founded, through the years of the English Civil War and the era of the Victorians, and on to the horrors and terrors of the twentieth and twenty-first centuries. Together these stories tell the tales not only of Crowford's inhabitants but also of the town itself.

This omnibus edition collects together, for the first time, 13 standalone titles from the Ghosts of Crowford series

AMY CROSS

BOOKS BY AMY CROSS

1. Dark Season: The Complete First Series (2011)
2. Werewolves of Soho (Lupine Howl book 1) (2012)
3. Werewolves of the Other London (Lupine Howl book 2) (2012)
4. Ghosts: The Complete Series (2012)
5. Dark Season: The Complete Second Series (2012)
6. The Children of Black Annis (Lupine Howl book 3) (2012)
7. Destiny of the Last Wolf (Lupine Howl book 4) (2012)
8. Asylum (The Asylum Trilogy book 1) (2012)
9. Dark Season: The Complete Third Series (2013)
10. Devil's Briar (2013)
11. Broken Blue (The Broken Trilogy book 1) (2013)
12. The Night Girl (2013)
13. Days 1 to 4 (Mass Extinction Event book 1) (2013)
14. Days 5 to 8 (Mass Extinction Event book 2) (2013)
15. The Library (The Library Chronicles book 1) (2013)
16. American Coven (2013)
17. Werewolves of Sangreth (Lupine Howl book 5) (2013)
18. Broken White (The Broken Trilogy book 2) (2013)
19. Grave Girl (Grave Girl book 1) (2013)
20. Other People's Bodies (2013)
21. The Shades (2013)
22. The Vampire's Grave and Other Stories (2013)
23. Darper Danver: The Complete First Series (2013)
24. The Hollow Church (2013)
25. The Dead and the Dying (2013)
26. Days 9 to 16 (Mass Extinction Event book 3) (2013)
27. The Girl Who Never Came Back (2013)
28. Ward Z (The Ward Z Series book 1) (2013)
29. Journey to the Library (The Library Chronicles book 2) (2014)
30. The Vampires of Tor Cliff Asylum (2014)
31. The Family Man (2014)
32. The Devil's Blade (2014)
33. The Immortal Wolf (Lupine Howl book 6) (2014)
34. The Dying Streets (Detective Laura Foster book 1) (2014)
35. The Stars My Home (2014)
36. The Ghost in the Rain and Other Stories (2014)
37. Ghosts of the River Thames (The Robinson Chronicles book 1) (2014)
38. The Wolves of Cur'eath (2014)
39. Days 46 to 53 (Mass Extinction Event book 4) (2014)
40. The Man Who Saw the Face of the World (2014)
41. The Art of Dying (Detective Laura Foster book 2) (2014)
42. Raven Revivals (Grave Girl book 2) (2014)

AMY CROSS

For more information, visit:

www.amycross.com

AMY CROSS

Printed in Great Britain
by Amazon